TIME FOR A SERIAL KILLER

A LIFETIME OF MURDER

R.K. MULLINS

UNTITLED

As David sat alone in the dimly lit office, his mind reveled in his past glories of writing excellence that won him the Pulitzer Prize for journalism years ago. David was a veteran criminal reporter. This entailed digging up information and reporting on the horrors held deep within the darkest recesses of humanity. The stories he wrote enticed and attracted readers. They held them spellbound, waiting for the next riveting episode in his weekly column. David didn't write about ordinary crimes; he specialized in serial killers. He uncovered the truths behind their art form—yes, each killer envisioned his ghastly act of murder as a work of art. David had helped the police track down more than ten killers in over five states. One case won him the coveted Pulitzer Prize.

As far as artists were concerned in this unique and bloody art form, William Stephen Martin would have been considered a premier artist in his field. William Stephen Martin had catapulted himself to the status of king of the serial killers, with a career spanning more than fifteen years, with over twenty-five victims.

Like most serial killers, William specialized in a predefined victim type.

He preferred young blond women with shy, introverted personalities. These type of women would become easy prey for William. He would follow them, learn their habits, their likes, dislikes, sorrows, and important information that would endear him to them. Through the exhaustive and relentless efforts of David Randolph Erwin, the police and the readers of his weekly article found these women held a close resemblance to Martin's first love. She was a young woman who had jilted William and left him standing brokenhearted at their wedding altar. This buxom blond beauty had stolen William's heart and left him a mere shadow of the man he was. She would become William's first victim in a long line of victims. How could Stacy Galleon have known her action and change of heart would bring poor William down a bloody road of death and torture? To date, Ms. Stacy Galleon's body has never been found. William alone knows where her remains are, and that information was buried with him.

David and the police questioned William all the way up to the final hour of his life. David had hoped William would disclose where he left Stacy's body prior to his execution, but he only left a clue hidden in his final words. "She is sleeping with my heart. She rests there." The police speculated Stacy Galleon was killed two weeks after she left him standing in front of the church they loved, the detective in charge of the case wrote in his final report. William was left standing there, betrayed by the woman he loved. A simple act of cold feet by Ms. Stacy Galleon pushed him over the edge and into a life of murder.

At the time of her disappearance, the police believed William had taken her from her parents' house in Albany, New York, and dumped her body in a nearby river. But without any evidence to hold him on, the case grew cold. Fifteen years later, David, searching for connections on other murders, led him to William Martin. Twenty-six weeks after David began his investigations, the police were finally able piece things together and arrested William Martin on twenty counts of murder with the help of David. William Martin himself confessed to another five victims the police and David had missed. There were five missing women now known to be dead. William told the police where they could find each one.

David's article held the reader's attention throughout the long investigation. At the end, they enjoyed reading the guilty verdict and death sentence William Stephen Martin received. The police thanked David for his exhausting efforts and admitted that William Stephen Martin would not have been caught if not for David. William Stephen Martin was executed on a stormy night in October. He had requested that the execution be held on Halloween; however, the court declined to grant him his request. At the hands of an expert marksman, Martin met his end.

David wrote, "A single bullet would bring William Stephen Martin's life to a painless end." This would be more consideration than Martin had given his victims. David wrote the last article in the long series of articles, calling for justice for the victims.

"Today one bullet entered one heart. Now one monster hides no longer in the darkened closets of our minds. The closet doors are now shut until the next monster enters the room. One bullet, one heart, one man, one story. This was all that was left for the readers to read. No longer would young blond girls need to fear for their lives. No longer would mothers and fathers fear the worst when their daughters were late coming home. The only thing missing from this conclusion were the screams of William Stephen Martin. His victims needed—nay, demanded—these screams be louder and more painful than their own. One bullet, one heart, ending the career of this monster. Justice was not served this day. The victims were not only robbed of their lives, now they were robbed of their justice. Justice of a monster being put through more hell than he had put them through. One bullet, one heart, one death, no victim cries left to be heard."

It has been more than six years now since David had written the articles that won him the Pulitzer Prize. Unable to find new monsters to keep his readers spellbound, he finds himself at a lowly newspaper. These days David reports on daily mundane things, like flowers blooming at the atrium or the new tiger being shipped to the zoo.

From time to time, David is able to find a story to sink his teeth into, but these cannot compare to William Stephen Martin. Now he finds himself holding on to past glories and reliving these days with whomever will listen. David still reaches out, trying to find a way back from the depths of nowhere, the brink of the destruction of his career, dreaming of the day when he breaks a new story to catapult his career back to the top. However, his publisher doesn't share his dreams of climbing back from the brink.

His publisher has warned him that if he cannot get a story worth reporting on, David will find himself on the streets yet again. This is not the first time David has had the threat of his employment dangling over his head. David had climbed to the top of the reporting world and now finds himself at the very bottom. In this small newspaper, there is little, if no, crime to report on; and the few crimes that are committed are handed to other reporters. David sees the chances of climbing back to the top far reaching at best, just long past glories and time passing him by. Serial killers are not that easy to find, and in the backwoods of Louisiana, they are even harder to come by. Most of the stories that David has followed have ended in the perpetrators being singular crimes, onetime events. For David, this has brought him to the bottom of his field and kept him there. Serial killers don't come seeking out reporters. They enjoy their work alone. It is not for display, and others are not permitted to pollute their art, thus making it harder to find them.

He is at a local paper of a small town in south Louisiana, reporting on local events that will never allow him the opportunity to scale the heights once again. Thus finds David sitting at his computer this late night, trying to find a story fitting of his skills. David scans the Internet, looking for any possible murders that may lead to the next William Stephen Martin. The sounds of the janitor's mop sloshing around in his mop bucket overpowers the sounds of David's fingers pounding out the keystrokes, searching the police files across the world, trying to locate the next great story. Stories like these don't just fall into the lap of the reporter; they must be sought out, discovered, and slowly cultivated to the point where they become a must-have story for the readers.

Readers are easy to lose. If the stories don't capture them from the very start, they will not return for more. If the stories hold them bound to the pages of the paper, they will return week after week to read the next riveting lines, to find out the great discoveries from the reporter. These are the only thoughts that enter David's mind. His publisher will not allow him the time to do this research—the needed research to find the next great story.

"Mr. Erwin, sorry to bother you."

"What is it, Jason? What is so important that you need to break the silence of my thoughts? What could you have to say that could possibly interest me? Come on, spill the beans, Jason. What do you have to say? Will it give me the story I need? Will it be a confession of guilt? I think not. But go ahead. Disturb my thought, end my career, and let's hear it. I can no longer wait. Please explain why you, a lowly janitor, a mop slinger, finds the need to disturb my thoughts."

"I am sorry, Mr. Erwin, but I finds this envelope that someone has slidded under the door with yous name on it. I thought it might be important. But me, a lowly janitor cleaning up the messes of people like you, should have known not to interrupt yous thoughts."

"Jason, I am sorry. I shouldn't have spoken like that to you." *I should have told that ignorant coonass to shut the fuck up. Hand me that and get out.* Slidded, yous, *damn, what uneducated words from an ignorant man. Let him clean up our messes. Let him feed his family on his meager wages. Maybe one day people like Jason will learn the importance of the work that they disturb and leave the educated man to his work. To bother me over a damn letter. A letter without the name of the sender. Well, what the fuck, let me see what this is all about. Maybe it will entice me in some small way.*

David holds the small uninteresting envelop and tears the glue-sealed flap open and pulls out the contents. David holds the paper close to the light of his desk lamp and reads the words handwritten on the page.

Mr. Erwin, I am writing to you in hopes that you might write my story. Tell the world of my life's work. For you see, I have been an admirer of your writing for some time now. I followed the articles you wrote that led to the capture of William Stephen Martin. Your words held me spellbound for those long weeks, and every week I could not wait until the next article came out to find out more of this artist's work. I admired his work more so than yours. I could not contact him, nor could I contact you until I was ready for your readers to learn of an artist greater than Mr. William Stephen Martin. His work came to an end way too soon. I believe he would have one day surpassed me in his brilliance. However, you ended his career way too soon. His end was not as it should have been. He should have had an end more fitting of his work. One bullet, one heart, isn't that what you wrote? One bullet, one heart, one man's work cut short. The fifteen years Mr. Martin spent on his art cannot compare to the forty-four years I have spent on mine. With my life coming to an end soon, I thought it was only fitting that my story and life's work be told by a master artist such as you. For most reporters, work is nothing more than words on blank paper. However, for you, the blank paper is your canvas, the words are your paint. Through this media, you bring light to the darkness of your reader's minds. Through you, your readers can live lives that are far from their own. Through your words, artists like me can bring their work to the light of day and show the embodiment of their work to the world. For you and your kind are the portal in which we work.

Most will never hear of us unless you write the words need to do us justice. Mr. Erwin, if my letter has enticed your imagination, then convey this to me in your next article. Bury it in the words of the flowery everyday events that you now cover. Simply say, "To my readers, thanks for all the letters of gratitude for the articles that I have written" and that you wish you could meet every reader and get to know their stories. With these words, I will know that you have the desire to meet me and to tell my story. However, if I find out that you have contacted the police or even shown this letter to a single soul, I will disappear, and my story will die with me, and my work will go unnoticed.

You see, Mr. Erwin, I am dying of cancer. My life will end in a few weeks at my own hand. I will not allow this dreaded infliction to consume me. I will end my life in a manner fitting an artist such as myself. I will look for these words in this Sunday's paper. If they are not found within your writings, then you will read of an old man found dead at the foot of the steps of your paper. Maybe it will be you who will write about this lonely old man who ended his life at the steps of the paper he loved.

One way or another, you will meet me. It is your choice as to how. Dead or alive, I have lived my life in the dark recesses of death and thus, dead or alive you will meet me. Story or not, you now must choose. I do so hope that your choice will be to write my story and allow your readers the advantage of learning of my art so that they, too, can appreciate the work that I have completed and the end that I have chosen. No court will ever see me, no jail will ever hold me, and no executioner other than me will end my life. The judgment is yours. Guilty is the verdict, death the sentence. The only thing to remain is the story to be told.

Sincerely,

An artist and a fan

Reading over the letter once more, David thought, *What a nut.* No way could this be true. No one in their right frame of mind could expect anyone to believe such blatant bullshit. Why anyone would dare think that such fanatical claims are worth writing about. The longer David sat and thought about the letter, the more he found himself wishing the possibility of such miraculous claims of forty-four years of death and destruction were true. Is there any chance the murderous claims are more than just the delusional dream of an old man reaching out for the smallest bit of attention as he nears his final days? To reach out in this manner must have taken some real guts; this alone might be worth time spent investigating his dark claims.

David sat and thought more and more, almost reaching the point of obsessing over the handwritten words. Finally, David decided that it was just the rather dark and sinister dream of a lonely person reaching out for attention. Somehow he or she must have not been able to gain through their life in any other manner. David wadded up the letter and tossed into the trash can beside his desk. Suddenly, Jason walked back into the room, spilling dirty mop water as he dragged his bucket behind him.

"Mr. Erwin, as I was headsin' to the janitor's closet, I spots someones walkens fast down the hallways. I starts to trys to catches him, but he rans into the elevator and the doors closed befo I coulds stops him. I thoughts it's best to come tells yous about it, when I spots another envelope on the floor by the doors. Not wantsin' to disturbs yous again, I lefts it there thinkens yous would finds it whens yous left. It's my times to goes homes, and it was still theres so here I am again. I knows yous don't like being interrupteds, but I figures this might has somethings to do with the other one, so I's betters brings it to yous."

David reached out and took the seemingly innocent envelope from Jason's hand. As Jason was walking away with his mop bucket dragging behind, David asked, "Jason, did you by chance get a good look at the man that you saw walking away?"

"No, Mr. Erwin. I couldn't see him too goods. He was wearing a long black coat with a hat like they uses to wear in the old days. So I's couldn't see his face or anything."

David tore open the envelope to find another single page waiting inside. The handwriting was the same as the first letter.

Mr. Erwin, by now you must have read my letter and come to the conclusion that I am a complete lunatic, or at the very least someone reaching out for attention. I dare say you more than likely have tossed the letter in the trash can beside your desk.

What, how could he know this? How long was he standing there watching me read the letter? This is nuts! Is he stalking me? Am I in some sort of danger from this lunatic?

And now, Mr. Erwin, you must be thinking that you are being stalked and that you are in danger. I assure you, this is far from the truth. I merely wish to impress upon you the seriousness of my first letter and how sincere it was. I can either become your best work or merely one of the small unnoticed pieces that you have been writing these past six years. The choice is up to you as to how this will end. The story of your life, or a sad little man dead at the foot of the last newspaper that dared to employ you. You know what I must see. I will be looking for the word of acceptance in what could be the last worthless piece of crap you will ever write. By this I mean you will either become the writer you once were or you won't. You decide, Mr. Erwin. You decide.

David reached for the letter wadded up in the trash receptacle by his desk and slowly retrieved it. As he was straightening the paper out to pour over it once more, he thought how someone he did not know could know so much about him. No one but the man who hired him knows that he used to be the greatest criminal writer; no one knew this. Or so he thought.

Damn, I wish he had given me another way to contact him. I hate kissing the ass of these ignorant fools. What to do, what to do? Should I contact the cops? Should I just throw this away and take it for what it seems to be—an attempt at getting some attention by a complete and utter nutcase? Why would he take the time to watch me read the first letter and throw it away? What might he do if I do not do what he asked? What else do I have to do, write another stupid article about some damn flower show? A new twist on how the winner cared for the roses over three years to bring them to the majestic glory of a blue-ribbon victory? What the hell, let's see where this takes me. I don't have anything to lose. And hell, I might just get a good human-interest piece out of this.

David sat there at his computer, typing away and trying as

hard as he could to pour emotions in to the words of the article for the Sunday edition, trying to make the best of this crappy story on the annual Gumbo cookoff held this morning and how the winner for the third year in a row was worried that she might not win. As she tried to sound humble and unassuming, she went on about how the competition was steeper this year than any other. People had come from as far as Texas to try to win the $1,500 grand prize and how most of them spent more than $2,000 to get there and compete. As David neared the end of his article, he pondered over the offer that was made to him in the letter. In his twenty-three years as a criminal reporter, David had received maybe two hundred letters of this kind; however, none had made the claims this author had made. David thought this could be his last chance to get back on top and win him a spot at the *New York Times* once again.

Once David was the premier criminal reporter at the *Times* and had the distinction of being the best in the business. David could pick and choose the stories he wanted, leaving the rags to the newcomers. The thought of being able to get back on top after six long years of failure and isolation in this desolate small-town paper was almost too much for him to bear. Every day he would call the bigger papers and submit his resume in hopes that someone would rescue him from his isolation. Could this letter be his salvation? Would this lead him to the light once again? Since David's start in the business twenty-three years ago as a young twenty-four-year-old reporter, green and just out of college, he had never kissed the asses of his readers in the way that the author of the letter was asking him to.

Concluding his article, David wrote, "To all my readers, I would like to thank you for your support and kind letters of encouragement. If it were not for you, my valued readers, I would not be where I am today. Thanks for everything, and I hope one day to have the pleasure of meeting each and every one of you. Please do not take this as a goodbye. Take it for a heartfelt thank you. I will continue to try to write articles you, my valued readers, are interested in reading." As David wrote the last few lines for the article, he found himself wishing this one would be the one to rescue him from his despair. How this would blow the mind of his publisher; never before had David wrote words of gratitude. This would be a complete surprise to her. *I will have to come up with some story that will allow her to believe I am sincere and wish only to thanks those dear readers. If I can't get her to believe me, she will not allow it to go out as is.*

The next morning, Barbra Watson, the owner and publisher of the paper, read David's new article. Upon completion of the article, Barbra called David into her office.

"David, what the heck is going on? I have never heard of you thanking your audience before. Don't take this the wrong way. I am not displeased with it. I am just wondering why now. Are you thinking of leaving us? Are you trying to break the news to me in this article? What's going on?"

"No, Barbra, I am not leaving. No other paper has contacted me. I just thought maybe it was time I showed appreciation to the readers that keep me employed. For far too long I have berated the readers, and I feel that this has added to my fall from grace. Readers need to know that they are appreciated from time to time. I spoke with a friend of mine in New York, and I was telling him that I was at my wit's end. No one would return my calls. My résumés were sent back unopened. What could I do? How could I be so far out of the mainstream and not be able to climb my way out? My friend told me that maybe I was meant to be here. Maybe I need to be humbled myself, lose the ego a bit. Learn what keeps us all in the business. I asked him what the hell he was talking about.

"The readers, my friend replied. The readers are our life's blood, not the stories. They give us the means to explore the world and through us they are able to live lives they otherwise could not. If it were not for our readers, then where would we be? The only difference between him and me, he explained, was that he knew the importance of the readers and showed his appreciation to them from time to time, to let them know it was their need to read that held control over us. And I, on the other hand, felt like they were a bother at best. It wasn't until he pointed that out that I was able to see what he was talking about. After I hung up the phone, I thought about what he had said and found he was right. I treated the readers as trash. As if they needed me instead of me needing them. Never thinking of who I was writing for, I thought my words were enough for me. Never did I consider the value of the readers. They are our life's blood. They keep us writing the stories that they want to read. I am a forty-seven-year-old man who thought he was God as far as journalism was concerned. So I guess I woke up and smelled the proverbial coffee and decided to let my readers know that they are the ones that are important and not I."

"Damn, I thought I would never hear you admit to that. I knew it to be true, but to hear you say it. *Wow.* I guess you would like me to let this go as is, without editing. Maybe I will. It should be said. Let the readers fall in love with the reporter. Let them learn that they are the stories. I think for once I have to agree with you. Don't let it go to your head, and I will send this to press as is. Let's see what comes of it. Let's see if the readers believe you."

Leaving Barbra's office, David thought, *Sucker. What an idiot. Damn, if I had known that all I had to do was kiss some ass and things would be easier, I might have considered it sooner. Nah, at least the article will be printed as is. Maybe I will get a great story from this and maybe not. Only time will tell.*

Monday night finds David sitting at his computer like any other night, searching for the elusive story to help him get back on top of the reporting world. To gain the attention of those publishers who once praised David for his writing skills and who won't even return his calls now. *Has-been*, they call him. *Washed up, finished*—these are the words he hears resonating in his ears. He is always searching for that one breaking story that will bring him back to the world he once loved. Searching but yet to find the one story that only he can write.

Again the silence was broken by Jason, his mop sloshing in his mop bucket. Once again, Jason interrupts the quiet thoughts of David. However, this time Jason was asked to disturb him if anyone or anything entered the doorway of the office.

"Mr. Erwin, there's another letter with yous name on it."

"Thanks, Jason. Thanks for all your hard work, and I am sorry for talking to you the way I did the other night. I was sort of rude and mean. I should not have said those things."

"Dat's okay, Mr. Erwin. I'm kinda used to it. I ain't no eduuuuuucated man. But I works hard and earns my keep, feeds my family, and that's all we need."

"Thanks again, Jason."

David held the now familiar gray envelope tightly in his fingers, hoping that it held information to whom and where the author was—two of the four *W*s that all reporters need to their write their stories. The two that David was now expecting to find within the pages of this new letter. Would these answers be waiting? Could this all have been a tease, or would David only find a cruel joke played at his expense? Ever so slowly, David pulled the letter from its gray home, unfolded the paper inside, and eagerly started to read.

Erwin, waiting on the street below you will find a black car with the windows painted black. This car will bring you to the place where our meeting will be held. Don't try to speak to the driver. He was given strict orders not to engage you in the smallest way. If you try to peek through the windshield, the driver will speed away, and you will have lost the only chance you have for this meeting. All that is needed from you is to get into the car and enjoy the food and wine left there for you. I have provided you with a few good books from my library. Enjoy them. The trip will take about two hours, and at no time will you be allowed to see where you are going.

If these terms are acceptable to you, please go swiftly to the waiting car. The driver was ordered to leave if you had not entered the car in ten minutes. This is the amount of time that it would take me to walk down the hall from your desk, enter the stairway, and make my way to the car. I am an old man, so I assume that you should be able to make it to the car quicker than I. As before, if you choose not to take advantage of this opportunity, then you and the police will find my body lying on the foot of the steps to your paper. With no explanation, no warning other than this one, no note, just my bloody body left behind. You should now be finishing this letter, and the car awaits. Leave or stay. Your choice. Tell my story, show the world my art, or leave it as is. The car waits.

Sincerely,

An artist and fan

David thought for only a second.

"This is nuts. I can't believe I am going to do this. I could be killed, or worse. What does this man want? What can he tell me? What stories are there hidden in his life? Even an old man might have a good story, if this is an old man."

Quickly, David ran to the stairs, hoping that no one was there to harm him. Afraid of losing the chance to redeem himself in the eyes of the journalism world, David had to take the chance. This was all for real. "Could this really be my chance? Could I really climb back from the pit of despair?" Slowly, David opened the heavy steel door to the stairway. He peaked around the door to find the stairs empty. "Shoo." His heart had almost stopped beating from the anticipation of what he would find. Man's imagination has always conjured up the greatest fears, pictures of demons that only the mind can invent. "Shoo." He was wiping the sweat from his brow, relieved to find the coast to be clear and no monsters under the stairs. Running down the stairs, David fell a few times, hitting his knees on the hard concrete floor, until he reached the main door to the lobby and the car waiting outside. Black as the night, the windows were painted. If it were not for the streetlights illuminating the car, David would not have seen it sitting there. The moon shined brightly in the clear southern Louisiana sky, giving him the feeling all might not be well should he continue down this road. Standing there with his hand on the door handle of the car, David thought of turning around, running back upstairs to his desk, and hiding under it. The driver of the car laid a hard-heavy hand on the horn, beckoning David to either enter or leave. The driver couldn't care less. He would get paid either way. David opened the door with his trembling hands; he had to use both hands because one was not allowing him the strength to pull the handle enough to open the door.

Not quite settled in his seat, the driver pulled away. Now off on their long two-hour journey, David noticed another gray envelope with his name printed on the front. Reaching for the letter, he saw the wine chilling in the wine bucket and a glass resting beside the wine, as if to be saying, "Relax, have a glass, unwind a bit." Just as a bartender might say as you walk into your favorite neighborhood bar. The pouring of the wine almost made David forget about the letter waiting on the seat beside him. Replacing the wine in its icy container, David reached for the letter. He took a sip of his wine before opening the gray envelope and pulling out the page hidden within.

Mr. Erwin, by now you must be asking yourself what you are doing. You might even have thought that you could be walking straight into the hands of death. Fear not. I am not out to do you harm. I can promise you that you will suffer no ill effects from meeting me. I am Randolph Cardigan.

"What, Randolph Cardigan, the previous owner of the paper? What, is this a joke?"

Yes, Mr. Erwin, your old boss. What a surprise. I am sure that you are swearing and using all sorts of foul language imaginable. But I guarantee you will not be disappointed in this meeting. You will receive the story of a lifetime. Sit back. Enjoy the wine. I have placed a selection of the world's best cheeses for you to sample, as well. I am sure these will not be wasted on your palate. I am sure that during your time spent in the New York journalism scene, you were introduced to some of the finer things that life has to offer. Enjoy all I have provided you with. Don't worry about offending the driver's ears. He is deaf. I will see you soon.

"What the fuck. Why all the damn secrecy? Why not just ask me to join him? What the fuck. What story could he have to offer me? He led me to believe that he was like William Stephen Martin. What a waste. Well, too late now. I might as well enjoy the treats he left me."

Halfway through the two-hour car ride, David had almost finished the fine cheese and wine when the car came to a stop. "It had only been one hour. Why are we stopping? We can't be there already. But maybe we are. I have been misled thus far. Why not the length of time the ride would take."

Reaching for the door handle once again, David rehashed the thought that this all could be nothing more than a rich old man hoping for some last-minute attention. What the hell, Randolph Cardigan did offer him a job when no other paper would have him. Why not humor the fantasies of the benefactor he had never met? This would be the least David could do to say thanks for the job. He had often wondered why this man would hire him sight unseen; and when he sold the paper two years ago, part of the deal was that the new owner would have to keep David on the payroll for no less than two years. David was the only employee Randolph had demanded the new owner, Barbra Watson, be kept on. He did not care if she fired the whole damn paper, as long as David stayed on. Randolph had sold the newspaper for health reasons, or so everyone was led to believe. And now David would find out the real reason for the sale and why he had never met Randolph Cardigan.

When the car door finally opened and David stepped out, he found himself facing an old run-down house. The porch looked as if it was ready to fall to the ground, as if placing one foot on a single plank would find the owner falling through and ending up on his ass. The rest of the house looked as if it had not seen a speck of paint in years. The house reminded David of the house from the old television series *The Addams Family* or *The Munsters*. It was in about the same condition as those old TV houses.

"This could not be the house of Randolph Cardigan." He couldn't live here. Maybe he was like an old recluse David had read about. Wealthy, but lived like a pauper. "Could this be the life of Randolph Cardigan? Is he such a recluse?"

Standing in front of the main door leading to the inside of the house, David saw an old door knocker much like those on old turn-of-the-century mansions. It looked as if it was made of solid brass, tarnished and weathered and in the shape of a scary old man with the knocker ring connected to the pointed Spock-like ears. David gently grasped the ring, pulled it back, and gave it a firm push forward. The knocker fell hard against the chin of the face, and David heard a loud bang as the two metals collided. The sound resonated throughout the inside of the house, and David was able to make out the sounds of soft footsteps coming toward the door. These soft footsteps made him believe that a woman was approaching. When the door slowly opened, he could see that his suspicions were correct.

A young lady appeared dressed in a skintight baby blue dress with small buttons ranging from her midsection up to her creamy white neck. Her hair was the color of autumn leaves and fell about her shoulders like the limbs of a weeping willow tree. As if David could ever notice how far up the buttons went, his eyes never made it past her ample breasts. David let his eyes wander up and down the thin beautiful frame of the young woman and finally fixed them on her waistline. He could barely make out lines where her panties lay, staring as if he could see clear to the feminine bounty that lay beneath her dress.

"Umm, sir, might I help you? If you took your eyes off my lower half and guided them upward, you might find that I have two eyes and a mouth. Now, if you would please stop staring at an area you can only dream about and address me in a respectful manner, maybe I can help you."

David reluctantly allowed his eyes to focus upward to gaze into her big beautiful brown eyes.

"Thank you, sir. Now may I help you?"

"Oh, I am sorry. Yes, I am here to see Mr. Cardigan. I was invited here to meet with him about a matter he wished to discuss with me."

"Please follow me this way, sir, and I will announce you."

As David followed the beautiful young auburn-haired woman, his eyes were fixated on her tiny round bottom.

"Sir, I would kindly ask you to take your eyes off my ass. I consider this to be rude and just what you think of women, so please do me a favor and keep your eyes fixed on the back of my head."

"I'll try, but I make no promises. You are a very beautiful woman, and it is so hard to keep my eyes where they belong." As if David thought his eyes belonged anywhere else. "But I will try."

David grinned slightly as if to hint that he had no intentions of doing as he was told.

Entering the rundown house, one would forget the outside of the house was dilapidated and fallen down. The hallway walls were covered with beautiful old turn-of-the-century wallpaper and reminded David of the plantations of old Louisiana. The walls on the right side were adorned with paintings from Monet, Michelangelo, Donatello, and some works that David didn't recognize. Fine tapestries hung on the left side, each depicting medieval battles. Knights with drawn swords, fighting dragons, and battling invaders saving fair damsels in distress seemed to be the story each was telling. A multicolored Persian rug ran the full length of the hallway. The designs swirled and swayed in many circular forms. They almost made David dizzy the way they flowed around and over each other. Peeking out from under the magnificent rug were beautiful old wooden floors, shimmering from what must have been their daily coat of wax. David tried ever so hard to see if the reflections from the floors would allow him the smallest of glimpses up the young woman's dress. He had hopes of seeing if she wore a thong or no undergarments at all. At the end of the hall stood two shining suits of armor, each holding battle axes, and swords hung from their waists.

They must have been the guardians to the entrance of the great room. The back of the great room held a set of majestic staircases, one leading off to the left and the other to the right. Each were adorned with carvings of vines and leaves that seemed to wrap all the way around the railings. Both met at the top and appeared to be leading off to where the bedrooms must be hiding. To each side of the great room were two large black sets of double doors, massive in size and extending from the floor and three quarters of the way up the fifteen-foot high walls. Each set of doors wore unique carvings. David wondered if the carving were some way to identify each room. The set of doors to the right had carvings of more knights. David thought, *What the hell is with all these knights?* The doors to the left adorned what appeared to be angels, or maybe mythological flying creatures of some type.

"This way, Mr. Erwin. Randolph is waiting for you in the library."

The young woman pointed to the large black doors to David's right. "It figures these would lead to the library," stated David.

The young woman glanced and smiled as she started to open the door. The heavy black doors were almost too much for the thin-framed woman to push open. She pushed what seemed to be all her weight on the door, and as it started to open, the hinges squeaked as if they hadn't seen even the slightest bit of oil in the long years the door hung there. Light dripped into the great room as the doors slowly opened. As David peered around the edge of the massive doors, he was able to see a larger room with bookshelves along every wall.

"This is the library, Mr. Erwin."

"Yeah, I would never have known if you hadn't told me. It wasn't like the books were a dead giveaway or something."

The young auburn-haired woman glared in David's direction, as if to say, "No one likes a smart ass." Every bookshelf seemed to be overflowing with books. David thought back to how the walls and floors were covered with beautiful art and if that was any indication of Mr. Cardigan's tastes in reading material. David thought that the books housed within these shelves must all have been first editions of the greatest literary minds of all times. David imagined sitting in the big straight-back brown leather chair, reading from the works of Poe, Whitman, and Mark Twain.

"Aw, to relax and lose one's self in the great works held in these shelves."

"Randolph, Mr. Erwin has finally arrived."

Randolph looked up from the pages of the book he was reading to notice David drooling over the books that were within the room.

"Thank you, Tamara. I see you appreciate the fine works of the masters, Mr. Erwin. I would have expected nothing less from a great writer such as you. Mr. Erwin, please have a seat."

As David approached the chair and started to lower himself down, Tamara asked, "Will you require anything else of me before I head off to bed?"

"No, Tamara, I think we will be fine. Is there anything else you need, Mr. Erwin?"

"No, sir. I think I am fine for now."

Tamara walked toward the door and, before leaving the room, turned around and said, "Mr. Erwin, I see you had no trouble keeping your eyes off my ass."

"Yes, ma'am. My eyes were busy elsewhere as it were. However, I was enjoying the view as you walked away. And I must say, what a view it is."

"That figures, Mr. Erwin. Pigs like you think a sensual female is nothing more than a prize to gain, a piece of meat to enjoy. Well, I hope you enjoyed your view, even though it wasn't put on this earth for your pleasure. Swine like you are never satisfied with the conquest of a single woman, and you must attempt to conquer us all. I am sure you have made a few great conquests in your time. However, you will not be adding me to your list. Your string of whores shall not be increased with me. You'll have to enjoy the imagination held in your own dark thoughts. Only your dreams of the pleasure that I could have brought to you will have to satisfy you. Good night, Mr. Erwin."

The door slammed shut with the force of ten large men. "That kind of force could not have come from such a delicate creature," David exclaimed. The vibrations of the door hitting against the doorjamb caused a few books to dislodge from their home and fall to the polished floor below. David rose from his chair and walked over to retrieve them and place them back on the shelves where they belonged. David noticed the name written on the cover of one of them—*Death of a Salesman*. This almost started David's dark thought of earlier to return. It was Tamara's footsteps echoing through the house as she ascended the staircase and made her way to her bedroom that stopped these thoughts from fully returning. David noticed the heaviness of the steps Tamara made —the footsteps of a woman with built-up anger issues toward men.

Mr. Cardigan looked over to David and said, "Mr. Erwin, you seem to know how to get under her skin. I would request that you not upset Tamara in such a way. She is a great gal. She helps me with just about everything. She cooks, cleans, and makes sure I take my medicines on time. She is more like a wife than an employee, just without the marital benefits. If not for her, I would be lost. So if you don't mind, treat her with the respect that you would wish your mother to receive. Even I look as she is walking off, especially when she is wearing tight blue jeans. *Wow*, what a sight. But I never let her catch me. She is what we used to call a feminist. Girl power and all that shit. Sometimes she catches me looking, and when she does, she shoots me a mean look. And every once in a while, she will give me a smile, and that smile is worth all the tea in China. I suspect as for the length of time you are here, I won't have the chance to enjoy that smile. I almost lost her once.

"I made the mistake of walking into her room while she was getting dressed. *Nice*. She almost quit then and there. I had to promise never to enter her room without knocking again and double her pay just to get her to stay. I still think I was set up. I know I knocked and could have sworn that she said come in. It was hard to argue with her while she was standing there in her birthday suit. It was all I could do to keep my eyes closed. All I could do was agree with everything she said and walk away like a whipped puppy with my tail between my legs. So please, Mr. Erwin, don't upset her. I would really like to keep her around a few more weeks without it costing me a bundle. Now please take a seat."

David sat back down in the brown leather chair and looked over to Randolph as if to say he was sorry for any problems he might have caused with Tamara.

"Mr. Cardigan, you look vaguely familiar. I know we haven't met before. However, I am certain that I have, at the very least, seen you somewhere before. You look like someone I should know."

"That could be, Mr. Erwin. You might have seen me in some tabloid paper somewhere or around at the paper before I sold it. Maybe even in New York, at one of those swanky newspaper conventions. It is possible that we have met and neither of us recall the time or place. Maybe we are the same person, but from different times. Who knows, Mr. Erwin, who knows?"

The same person but from different times. What a full-blown nut ball, David thought.

"Why have you called me here, Mr. Cardigan? Why the elaborate ruse? Your letter led me to believe a killer wanted tell his or her story. Now I think that maybe you just want someone to talk to. I am not sure why this meeting could not have been held back at the paper. Why contact me in such secrecy? Why mislead me, get my hopes up? Why make me think a lifelong killer was out there, and his story was mine? Why, Mr. Cardigan? Why?"

"Well, first things first, please call me Randolph. This Mr. Cardigan shit is for the birds. It makes me feel old. I have Father Time to remind of that, and I don't need any other gentle reminders. Life is the only game none of us get out of alive. We enjoy what we can. Take the small pleasures in bits and pieces when they come. Life disappoints us all. Why should you not be disappointed now, or will you be? I do have story to tell, and you're the only person that will be able to write it and do it justice. I thought of getting a reporter who enjoys the status you once did, but why when I have the best in the biz at my fingertips. Why let some hack screw it up? You are the best in the biz, or at what you used to report on. That is why I chose you for this story, for my life story, Mr. Erwin. That is why."

"Randolph, please call me David. Like you, all this sir shit makes me want to hurl. I am the best criminal reporter in the business, but it sounds to me like you want someone to write your biography. And if that is the case, then you might want to call someone else. This is not my forte."

"You maybe be correct, David. Maybe so. I wanted you, and you I have. No one else will write this. If you choose not to write my story, then it will go unwritten. You will find that the promise I made in my letter will be carried out. I do have cancer—lung cancer, to be exact. A product of some ninety years of smoking, and I will be dead within a few months. So you see, David, I really have nothing to lose by taking my own life. And I will not allow this dreaded affliction to totally consume me. I will win this time and go out on my own terms. So give a dying man his final request and write this for me. I promise, you will not be disappointed, and you will be well compensated for all your time and efforts."

"Well, Randolph, the compensation isn't the issue, and I believe you know that."

"True, David. I know what you want most of all. You want redemption. You want back on top of the business you so love. I can't promise you that will happen. However, I can promise you this will bring you closer than you have been in years. It is late, and I am tired. So I will say good night and see you at breakfast in the morning. Sleep well and ponder the offer. Let me know your answer at breakfast. Also, please make some kind of suggestion as to the price you want. That's right, David. It is a blank check. Write it for what you wish. Just tell my story."

"Good night, Randolph. Sleep well. You will have my answer in the morning."

As Randolph walked toward the door entering the great room, he turned and looked back at David with the begging eyes of a small child.

"David, the library is at your disposal. Look through the books. All of them are first editions, no copies or fakes. Enjoy them. Maybe you'll find one that will help you decide to take this task. And please take any of the rooms upstairs. Just don't try to open the two at the end of the hall. Those are mine and Tamara's, and hers is always locked. I leave mine unlocked in hopes that one night she might walk through the door and surprise me. Wishful dreams of a dying old man."

As the large heavy door closed behind Randolph, David stood there, thinking that he must have been crazy to think that a writer of David's quality and status would bother to write this dribble for him. David started walking toward the bookcase by the fireplace when he saw a book sitting on the end table beside the chair where Randolph was sitting. David was curious to see what kind of book Randolph might have enjoyed reading. David leaned over and picked it up. *Time Killer* was the title on its spine, but the author's name wasn't there. An unknown author of a book he had never heard of. David flipped it open to the cover page, only to find it blank. *Time Killer. Weird*, thought David, *a book with no words, no author, blank, everything blank.* Was this a book that Randolph had pondered writing, maybe? This whole thing was a bit strange for David.

"Strange indeed. Everyone off to bed before eight o'clock with no explanation of this whole damn thing. No clue as to why I am here, the real reason, not this fanciful one of a book that Randolph spoke of. What the hell, maybe I should just get the driver to take me back to the office; but if I go back now, I won't learn anything, and I will leave empty-handed. Going through all this and not getting anything in return, what a waste. Left standing here talking to myself like a complete madman. Okay, I'll give Randolph one more chance, and just maybe I will get something for my troubles."

David looked over the books nestled in the bookshelf beside the majestic fireplace. "*Time Machine, Executioners Song, Death of the Roman Empire.* Crap, all crap. Nothing worth reading! *Time for a Serial Killer, Time Twister.* All crap. Isn't there anything worth reading? Damn. Wait, *Time for a Serial Killer.* Maybe this one."

David reached for the book and again noticed there was no author listed on the spine of the book. "Not again." Just like David thought, the pages were empty just like the one on the end table

"How weird!" David turned the book over to see if there was any type of description on the back. *Aw, at least there is a brief piece on the back.*

"June 7, 2010. He arrived at the house with no knowledge of what awaits him. Would he stay to learn what was in store? Would he listen and see how his life would change?"

"What the fuck. June 7. Damn, that's today. Is this written here on this back cover me? Could this be a trap of sorts? What was I thinking? No way am I staying here and wait for my demise like a lamb in a slaughterhouse."

David ran to the large black doors leading to the great room and stopped. He slowly opened one, trying ever so hard to keep it from creaking. Once he entered the great room, he made a mad dash for the front door and threw it open. Standing there on the rundown porch, he looked around trying to find the car that brought him here. With only the light from the thumbnail-shaped moon to see by, David could just barely see that the car was no longer in the driveway. He looked down the length of the house and saw a small shed that looked like it could be a garage. His hope rose high, thinking they must have parked it there. David could barely see, but it appeared the building was in the same condition as the outside of the main house—rundown, almost in ruins. He could make out what seemed to be double doors, doors large enough for a car to fit through. "Yeah, baby, that's the place. They had to have parked it there."

Running to the large double doors, David tripped over a cypress stump that stood between the main house and the shed. The wet mud attached itself to David's pants like a baby to its mother's breast. As David reached the shed, he saw a few windows on the side of the all but collapsed building. He stopped long enough to peer inside to see if the car would be hidden within. He looked in through the dirt-coated panes of glass, trying to view the content inside. David took his shirtsleeve and dipped in the murky water of a nearby mud puddle in hopes that the water would clean off enough of the grime to allow him a small glimpse inside. He rubbed the mud-soaked sleeve on the dirt-caked glass, only to turn in it into a mud-coated pane of glass. David became more frustrated with every circular wave of his arm. Taking his dry sleeve, David wiped at the muddy glass to clear away a small section of the murkiness. As he pushed his hand to the glass to create a tunnel to see through, David hoped he climbed ever so higher. "Maybe now I can see." Placing his face squarely in between his hands, David peered inside. David squeezed his face tighter and closer to the glass, only to find total darkness peering back at him. "Nothing, nothing but the darkness, damn it! Nothing but darkness. Can't I catch a break?" With his hopes seemingly dashed and lying broken on the ground at his feet, David walked to the double doors that lay waiting at the front of the shed.

"This is utter madness." David sighed. He reached out and grasped the rust-coated handle and gave it a mighty tug. Shaking the door with all his might, David tried to get it to budge. David realized it was as futile effort. Not allowing these setbacks to detour him, David walked around the garage, looking for any opening to which he might be able to see through. Any opening that would allow him to view the contents held inside. Finally, he found one solitary broken pane of glass with a small piece missing. He pressed his face close to the broken glass and strained his eyes to see what was waiting within. "Maybe if I allow my eyes to get used to the darkness, I can see." David stood there. waiting for his eyes to adjust in hopes he would be able to see something, anything. Suddenly, small shapes seemed to appear. At first, David was able to make out what looked to him like an oil container, then a gas jug. Next, as he looked around with his newly focused eyes, he saw a crescent wrench, a screwdriver, and a hammer. "Yes, finally I can see something. It's about fucking time. There, right there, I can see it. Wait, it isn't the black car that brought me, but it will surely do." David's patience was paid off as he was amazed to see what looked to be an old sixties model Ford Fairlane hidden inside. David could barely see that the car didn't appear to be in the greatest of shape, but it would do in a pinch. "Hell, I bet it doesn't even run. Trapped! Damn, trapped."

As David stood there with his dreams of escape seemingly dashed, his imagination started running wild yet again. He had thoughts of bloody axes and kitchen knives. Would the police find his bullet-riddled body lying in a muddy ditch somewhere? "Am I to be murdered? Was all of this just a misguided attempt to kill me? Wait, you damn fool. Just wait a second. Reason this out. Don't let childish nightmares and fears rule you here. Think it through. Mistakes are made when you fail to think things through."

Thinking for a second, David concluded that this old sickly man couldn't be out to kill him. He could barely gather the strength to make his way to his bedroom. He surely couldn't kill him. "What are you afraid of, David? What the hell, letting your imagination run wild like a six-year-old child. Have you lost all your backbone? Courage, man, courage. Once you were scared of nothing, no one, and now you are letting the night and dark thoughts of your own demise rule you. This isn't the man you once were. This isn't the man that used to track down killers and help bring them to justice. Get a grip. You're better than this."

Convincing himself that his life really wasn't in danger, David headed back to the house.

"David, ole boy, you are really this silly and childish, wasting your time letting things get to you like this. What are you, four? Allowing images of my death to enter my head, how foolish can one man be."

David returned to library and continued to search for a book that would lull him to sleep. "Aw, here we go. *A Tale of Two Cities*. This should do it. If this boring ass thing can't knock me out, nothing can."

Settling back down in the high-backed brown leather chair, David began reading. Soon he found his eyelids getting heavy. "How boring. I guess I should go upstairs and find myself a room for the night."

Climbing to the top of the staircase, David could hear sounds coming from one of the rooms at the end of the hallway. As he moved closer, he could make out that the sounds were coming from Tamara's room. Sighs and moans, the deep sounds of two people in erotic rapture. "That old fart, he's getting on with his hired help." David moved closer to Tamara's room, trying to see if he could get close enough to hear more. Standing just outside her door, David could clearly hear her moaning and groaning as if she was all but ready to explode. He leaned over, trying to peek through the keyhole, hoping to catch a glimmer of two bodies intertwined in mad passionate love, the raw animalistic actions that he himself wished he could enjoy.

"Now to bang that babe would be something. Wow."

He could just make out Tamara sitting on the edge of her bed. Her cream-like skin shining for the perspiration dripping down her body, his view was blocked by the wooden post stretching up to the canopy above the mattress. "Damn, bedpost. If not for that, I could see her tits." Just then, Tamara reached for a pink terrycloth bathrobe and draped it around her body. She stood up and started walking toward the door. David quickly rose and softly walked toward the room next to Tamara's and reached for the doorknob. Just then, the door to Tamara's room swung open.

Tamara poked her head around the doorframe to see David standing just outside the door of the room next to hers. She shot him a dirty look. "Were you just at my door, Mr. Erwin? Were you trying to get a cheap thrill, catch a sneaking peek at me? I wouldn't put it past a pig like you."

"Tamara, you only wish I would do something that immature. I'm not a sixteen-year-old boy looking to get my jollies from cheap glance. No matter what you think of me, I am not the oinker you think I am. I am deeply hurt that you would believe I would stoop so low as to peek through the keyhole of your door and get a cheap thrill, as you call it. If I were to do something so despicable, your bedposts would block any good view I might have anyway."

"Mr. Erwin, you are the swine I think you were."

Shooting David a dirty look, Tamara walked back into her room and slammed the door behind her. David turned the heavy knob to his room and slowly opened the door, wishing that Tamara would reenter the hallway and rush to his arms. "Time to retire for night, ole man. Get a good night's sleep and listen to Randolph for a bit tomorrow and be on my way." The room reminded David of the soft Southern rooms depicted in the old movie *Gone with the Wind*. A large king-size wooden bed with colorful flowery bedspread adorned the bed. Four delicately carved posts stood at each of the four corners of the bed. Each was carved with images of flowers and stems slowly rising form the square block at their base and scrolling upward to the ceiling. With a large Shaker wardrobe set in the corner of the room, the entire room was adorned with antique hardwood furniture from the Shaker period. Only the bed seemed to be from an earlier time. The walls were covered with more of the same old tapestries.

"Damn, what's with these rugs? What is with this guy and his fetish for knights killing dragons and other knights? Randolph must have a death fetish or something." For a moment, David's thought drifted back to the old man and him trying to kill David.

David broke out laughing. "I can't believe I let my imagination take over me like that."

David dropped his clothes at the foot of the bed and climbed in between the covers and reached for the book he started reading in the library, all the time wishing that Tamara would walk into his room and give him the attention she was giving Randolph. "Wait a second, where was Randolph? Could she have been alone the whole time? Could she have been getting that kind of pleasure from her own hands?" With the sweet images of his vivid imagination of Tamara's hands caressing her body and bringing her to ecstasy, David was soon fast asleep with a huge smile on his face, as if to be dreaming of bringing Tamara to the point she has seemingly brought herself to.

The next morning, David was awoken to the sweet smells of food cooking and coffee brewing. "Yes, coffee." Ever so slowly, David rose from his slumber and gathered his clothing from the floor where he had left them the night before, wrinkled and lumped together like two puppies asleep on the foot of the bed. "Damn, having to wear the same shit as yesterday. Where's that shower? At least I can wash the sleep from my eyes." David made his way down the hallway, opening each and every door until he finally found the bathroom. "About damn time." David went into the room to find more of the same medieval décor as in the rest of the house. "Shit, I was hoping for something other than this shit. What's with this man? Nothing but death and dying surrounds him. I know he's dying, but this morbid shit can't make his fate any easier to take."

David threw his clothes on the floor of the bathroom. As he turned to climb into the old bathtub, he noticed it was one of those old lion's foot type tubs with a large round silver-polished showerhead. "I hope this damn thing works." David reached for the hot and cold knobs and turned them until he reached the desired water temperature. "Aw, this will do." David showered and stood before the mirror, wondering what he was still doing there. Why hasn't he left yet? "When I see Randolph, I am going to let him know I am not interested in writing his so-called story. He needs a shrink, not a writer, and I don't have time for this psycho bullshit. I am not going to fill any of my time writing the drivel he might think is worthy writing."

David followed his nose downstairs and turned toward the area behind the staircase. Behind the massive staircase, a set of doors were hidden from view of the main greeting room he had entered in from the night before. David opened the doors to find the dining room. As he entered and looked around, he was disappointed to find nothing there—no coffee, no eggs, nothing. "Damn it, followed my damn nose only to find nothing. Not one damn egg, piece of toast, nothing. Where's the fucking coffee?" At that very moment, Tamara walked into the room with a coffee pot in hand. "You're a lifesaver, Tamara. Thanks for the coffee. Is Randolph around anywhere?"

"No, Mr. Erwin. Mr. Cardigan has left to keep his doctor's appointment. He always has to see the doctor on Tuesdays because of the cancer. He always has his chemotherapy treatment on Tuesdays and Thursdays. He should return by one o'clock, which is the time he usually get back from the doctor's."

"Thanks, Tamara."

"Are you hungry, Mr. Erwin? I have breakfast ready if you're ready."

"Oh, I am ready, young lady. I am more than ready. Aw, you meant to eat. Yeah, that too. If there's nothing else you wish to offer, I guess breakfast will have to do."

"Mr. Erwin, there is nothing that I would ever want to offer you, unless it was poison to put in your coffee. That, Mr. Erwin, is about all I would enjoy giving you."

"Tamara, please, you know you want me in the worst way. You know that I could make you scream with pleasure like no other man has before."

"Mr. Erwin, you are assuming that other men have had the chances with me that you will not. You know what they say, Mr. Erwin. Assumption is the mother of all fuckups. How narrow-minded of you, Mr. Erwin, to even think that I want a man and discount the fact that I might want women instead. These days, a woman can enjoy the warmth and tenderness of another woman as well as a man. This alone proves just what a pig you are."

"With that ass and those tits, you're a lesbian? I find that hard to believe. There must have been some man somewhere that has tasted your pleasures. It can't be true that you are a muff diver and not a stump sucker. Please tell me this is false. Please tell me that all your words are lies and that somewhere there is a man waiting for you. Please tell me this, or at the very least let me try to show you what you have been missing. Who knows, I might even convert you to a life of normal sexual relationships."

"Mr. Erwin, there is absolutely no hope for you. None whatsoever. I will leave the conversation at this point and leave you to your dirty, disgusting, perverted thoughts."

The sound of the sterling silver serving platters rang throughout the dining room as Tamara let it fall from her hands to the table below. David stuck one finger in his ear and gave it a shake, as if to clear the ringing from his ears. "Damn, that woman turns me on."

David sat at the end of the massive dining room table. It reached from one end of the dining room to the other. "This thing must be fifteen feet long." The deep, rich dark wood looked as if it was from an old English castle. David could imagine knights, ladies, and lords sitting around it, gnawing away on legs of lamb and large turkey legs. The table was decorated with three large vases filled with long-stemmed roses and baby's breath. "Baby's breath? Looks like weeds to me."

David grabbed a plate and filled it with bacon, three sunny-side up eggs, an English muffin, and poured a cup of coffee. As David sat there eating, he couldn't help but let his mind wander, imagining the type of stories that Randolph would unload on him. "I bet any stories Randolph would talk about couldn't be worth writing about.

"I know elderly people like to ramble on about days gone by. Reliving their past glories, business conquests, women that they have had, things like. I will let him talk for a few hours or a day to humor him, and then tell him I am going back to the office and write his story and then forget it once I leave."

David sat, eating his breakfast and laughing about the tall tales Randolph would bestow on him. How would he be able to stay awake through the long horrific hours with an old man rambling on and on and on. David dipped a piece of English muffin into the runny bright-yellow yolk of his eggs, wondering how he could get out of this without offending Randolph. Just then, Tamara walked into the room.

"Mr. Erwin, are you almost finished with you breakfast? I would like to clean up and get to my other tasks on my daily list. With you being here, it is putting me behind a bit."

"Tamara, I will be done in just a few minutes. Will you join me for a cup of coffee while I finish up? Your company would be greatly appreciated, and your sweet voice will break the silence of my thoughts. So please, sit with me. I promise to keep the conversation clear and away from any sexual innuendos. I won't even comment about you in any way."

"I know this will be a mistake, but I will sit with you for a bit until you have finished up. However, if you stray from your promise, I will leave after slapping the shit clear out of you. If this is agreeable, I will keep you company for a while."

"Great, you will see I can be a good boy if I want to."

"We'll see, Mr. Erwin. We shall see."

"So how long have you been with Randolph?"

"Well, I started with Mr. Cardigan about two years ago, right after he found out he had cancer. I met him at the grocery store, of all places, I was a cashier. I waited on him every week when he would come in and get his TV dinners. I finally got up the nerve to tell him what I thought of his eating habits. He would always buy the same ones week in and week out—turkey with dressing, meatloaf with mashed potatoes, and fried chicken. Never trying any of the others, never buying any fresh fruit or vegetables, nothing he would have to prepare and cook. That kind of diet is nowhere close to being healthy. After I berated him over his eating habits, he asked if I knew how to cook and if I had ever thought about doing something else, or if was I happy in my chosen profession. 'Profession. This isn't a profession, it is just a job' was my reply. He then offered me this job with more money than I had been used to making. As you know, the Walmart doesn't pay very well, so I couldn't see myself turning the offer down, and to have a nicer place to stay to boot made it a no-brainier for me."

"You were a Walmart cashier? I picture you as a nurse or as some sort of well-educated nutritionist or something."

"Well, I have a Master's Degree in Business Administration, but once I got into the workforce, I found out that it really wasn't my cup of tea. I just couldn't keep working for a system that fed off the suffering of others. The entire business world feeds off of man's inhumanity to man. The whole point of business is to increase profit in any way possible. If people have to suffer to meet the projected expected profits, then so be it. I just couldn't take it any longer and gave it all up. Walmart wanted me to be a manager, but I turned it down to work the front and serve those that served the business world."

"Well, I never expected that you were a woman of business. It just never occurred to me that you were that type of person. I saw you more in the medical profession or something along those lines."

"Mr. Erwin, you just don't seem to think past your first impressions, it would seem."

"Tamara, it just didn't seem to fit your personality. That's all I meant. I know you to be a bright and intelligent lady, and definitely an educated one. But business? Nah, that just didn't fit."

"Mr. Erwin, nothing seems to fit when it comes to you. One minute you're a smug, assuming woman-chasing pig, and then you switch gears and give off the appearance that you might actually give a damn about something other than your own animalistic needs."

"Tamara, please, would you call me David? This Mr. Erwin shit has got to stop. I am not that old, and nor do I desire this lack of familiarity. So please, call me David."

"We'll see, Mr. Erwin. We'll see. It took me the better part of six months to get comfortable enough to call Mr. Cardigan by Randolph. Why should it take any less time for you? I'm not at all sure if I even want to call you anything yet, and I am certain that I don't like you."

"Why, Tamara, not like me? What is there not to like? I am a loveable fuzz ball. Everyone who knows me loves me."

Tamara looked at David as if to say, "Who do you think you're kidding?"

"I am not at all the man you seem to think I am. I am gentle, kind, loving, honest, faithful, hell, you couldn't find a dog more loyal than me. What is there not to like about me? I am all this and much, much more; and for the most part, I am horny, and you need to take care of that for me."

"I knew it. I knew you couldn't keep your word and stay clear of any sexual remarks."

"Remarks? I made no remark. I made a comment that is surely based in fact. I am horny, and you are here and I am here. Randolph won't be back for a few more hours, and I have nothing else to keep me busy. Why can't we enjoy each other's bodies and bring each other some much-needed pleasure?"

Tamara got up from the table and reached her hand back behind her head and let it fly. The sound of her hand slapping against the side of David's cheek echoed throughout the dining room. It was loud enough to have been heard all the way upstairs into the bedrooms.

"Damn it, Tamara. Why the hell did you do that? Shit, it hurt!"

"I told you when I sat down that I would slap the shit out of you if the conversation took a turn toward sex, and I am a woman of my word, Mr. Erwin. Now give me your plate and get out of my damn sight before I hit you again. Remember this, Mr. Erwin. Remember it well, for if you ever talk to me like this again, I will do much worse than just slap you."

Tamara grabbed the coffee cup, plate, and silverware and headed toward the door of the kitchen. "Mr. Erwin, I hope you know I will be letting Randolph know about this when he returns. I am sure he will not be very happy to hear of this and will ask you to leave the house. And if he doesn't, then I will leave until you are gone."

Before David could say a word, Tamara walked through the door of the kitchen and slammed it behind her.

"Damn, that girl is hot. I better find a way to make things right with her before Randolph gets home. What am I thinking? This is my way out of here. Let her tell him then. Maybe I can leave and get back to the same ole everyday bullshit."

With the sounds of the door slamming shut still echoing in David ears, he pushed himself away from the table and walked toward the door leading back to the staircase. As he opened the large heavy doors, he could hear the footsteps of Tamara walking up the stairs.

"Damn it, I can't believe I am going to do this. I never apologize to anyone, and now am going to do it twice in one week. What the hell is wrong with me?"

David quickly walked out the door and started walking up the stairs and down the hallway toward Tamara's room. He reached out and laid a heavy fist on the door and started to knock.

"Come in."

David slowly opened the door as if halfheartedly dreading what might be waiting for him on the other side.

"Tamara, I wanted to say I am sssssss...what the."

Tamara stood at the foot of her bed with nothing on but a smile.

"Tamara, what is this? Was the slap and all that other shit just an act?"

"No, I wasn't acting. You really pissed me off."

"Then why are you letting me in your room, and you're buck naked. I just don't get it."

"What is there to not understand? In all the excitement and the heat of the moment, I got aroused. What is so hard to understand about that?"

"So you want me to fulfill your needs, or something like that?"

"No, I am going to take a cold shower, and I suggest you do the same."

"Well, I am at a loss for words. And trust me, this is something that never happens. Anyway, I wanted to tell you I was sorry. I was very bad, and you really didn't deserve that from me or anyone else."

"You're just trying to save your own ass. You don't mean a single word of it."

"No, really, I am truly sorry, and I don't give a rat's ass if Randolph kicks me out or not. It doesn't matter to me either way. I stand to lose nothing if he keeps me here or if he kicks me out. And by all means, please go ahead and tell him. Please do. It will save me the trouble of having to come up with some lame excuses to get out of this shit. So please tell him."

"Mr. Erwin, would you please turn around and leave. I wish to take that shower now. I'll decide later whether or not to tell Randolph. But for now, just get the hell out and stop staring at my breasts."

The heavy door slammed shut behind David as he entered the hallway. "Damn, she is hot, and man oh man, what nice tits."

"I heard that, Mr. Erwin!"

David walked to his room in hopes of Tamara following him there for a little late morning romp. As his door slowly opened, David glanced back toward her room, almost stalling there, waiting, hoping, dreaming of Tamara walking toward him to make his morning. "I wish she would come out right now. I would take her for the ride of her life." Standing there for what seemed to be ten minutes, David finally walked into his room and shut his door. Walking over to the window, David's thoughts moved back to Randolph and the type of stories he might impart to him.

"I really wish I could find a way out of this. I'm sure Randolph isn't the type of man who would take no for an answer. How or what could I do to get him to let me just go back to the paper and forget this shit?" David sat down on the edge of the bed, straining his brain for the answer to this question. "I got it. I'll tell him that Tamara and I had a very deep argument over her having sex with me, and she threatened to quit if I didn't leave the house. He wants to keep her here more than me, so I am sure this will work. He might get pissed, but fuck it, I want out of here, and this might be my only way." Settling back on the bed, happy with his newly formed plan, David started drifting off to sleep.

Just as his eyes seemed to shut for a nice calming nap, the silence was interrupted by the sound of a car driving up. David climbed to his feet and went over to the window to see if Randolph had returned. He looked out to see a cab pulling up and Tamara getting in and leaving. "Damn, alone in this old house and awakened from a nice slumber. What now?" David tried lying back down, but sleep was to escape him this time. "Just my damn luck. I can't get back to sleep. Where's that damn book? Maybe it will help me like last night." Reaching for the book on the end table, he started reading, hoping for the knockout punch it delivered the night before.

"This shit is just too damn boring. I didn't like it when I had to read it in high school, and I like it even less now. Maybe I can find something else to read. Maybe the morning paper is around her somewhere." David left his room and headed for the library for something better to read. As he was walking down the hallway toward the staircase, something made him look back, and he noticed that Randolph's bedroom door was open. "That's funny, I am sure it wasn't open when I came up here. I wonder if Tamara left it open for some reason." David walked down the hall to Randolph's room and peeked inside the room. Randolph's room was decorated much in the same manner as the other bedrooms David had been in, with a four-poster Victorian bed, Shaker dresser, wardrobe, and end tables. David noticed a piece of paper lying on the end table. He walked over to see what information it might have that he could use to his advantage.

Dear Mr. Cardigan, this is to inform you of the test result from the follow-up tests your physician ordered on May 16, 2010. As your physician had instructed, we are writing to let you know that the chemotherapy has not yet shrunk the tumors located in the first and third quadrant of you right lung. Further testing also showed the tumors located in your left lung have doubled in size. We have sent our findings and recommendation to your physician, and he will go over the options with you at your next appointment. However, as we were also instructed by your physician to disclose these findings with you and our recommendation, we are recommending your treatments be increased to twice a week with heavier doses of chemo. A very aggressive approach is needed in your case to shrink the tumors. With the size and location of the tumors and your advanced age, we cannot recommend surgery to remove the masses as we feel this will only open you up to more infections and needless trauma.

Sincerely,

Robert M. Starling, MD

"Shit, the old fucker is dying. I don't know what to do now. Should I stay and humor him for a few days? Hell, I hate being put in this spot. If I leave, then I look like a complete asshole that cares for no one. If I stay, I might lose the only job I have and waste time I really don't want to waste." David left Randolph's room and left the door slightly ajar as he had found it. He didn't want it to appear as if he had ever been in the room. Walking down the long stretch of hallway to the stairs, David's mind kept drifting back to the letter from Dr. Starling. "Damn, how it must feel to know you're dying and there is not one damn thing you can do to stop it. That has got to be the worst thing ever." David reached into his shirt pocket, pulled out a cigarette, and lit it. Drawing the smoke deep into his lungs, he stopped for a second and looked at the burning ember. "What the hell, I am smoking just after reading the news poor Randolph had received. I must be totally nuts."

David put the cigarette up to his lips, took another puff, and inhaled the gray smoke deeply into his lungs. David had not noticed the ashtrays that were standing at the top of the staircase the night before. "How handy, ashtrays. I wonder if they had been there the entire time. Surely they didn't just appear." David searched the back of his mind to see if he remembered the two swords with golden platters standing there. At first glance, they didn't appear to be ashtrays, but what else could they be with cigarette butts lying in them? "Yeah, they were here last night. I just didn't pay that much attention to them. They are rather unique." The ashtrays stood at the right height, David thought. "I don't even have to bend down to put out the smoke. But damn, what's with the medieval shit? Everything either has a damn knight, dragon, or swords motif about it. I got to ask Randolph what his fascination with this shit is when he gets back."

As David walked back to his room, he heard the faint sound of the car pulling up in the driveway. "Aw, Randolph is back. Maybe we can get to the bottom of this make-believe shit and I can get my ass out of here."

As David heard the front door creak open, he spun around and stood at the top of the staircase, waiting to see if Randolph was heading to his room or the library. "If he goes to the library, I'll wait a few minutes and then go down for our talk."

Randolph was escorted into the massive center room by the driver. "Sir, will you be needing me any more tonight?"

"No, Justin. I think I will be able to manage from here. Thanks for your help today."

The driver turned and went out the front door and closed it behind him. As the echo of the door closing started to fade,

Randolph walked over to the library and turned the handle opening the door. "David, would you care to join me for a drink and a smoke?" David stood there as if he hadn't heard Randolph. "Please, David, let's not pretend you're not there. We both are too old for childish games. So at your convenience, please join me in the library, and I'll start telling you about the life I've lived. And you can decide whether or not this is worth your time. If not, I'll pay you for your time and have my driver return you home in the morning."

David stood there for a second. "Damn, how did he see me?" Then he slowly started down the stairs. As David approached the library door, he saw Randolph had left it open. Slowly reaching out for the knob, David heard Tamara's voice. "Mr. Cardigan, what would you like for supper this evening?"

"Something light, Tamara. Maybe gumbo."

"Seafood or chicken?"

"Chicken will do nicely. Thanks."

David pulled the door open. Walking in, he cleared his throat to announce his presence. "Come in, David, come in. Tamara is going to make her wonderful chicken and sausage gumbo for dinner." David walked over to the empty chair beside Randolph and sat down.

"Great, Mr. Cardigan. I haven't really had good gumbo in a while."

"You're in for a real treat then. Tamara has won a few cooking contests with her gumbo."

"I'm looking forward to it, sir. Randolph, was Justin the driver that brought me here?"

"No, why do you ask?"

"I was just wondering, is all."

"No, Justin is my daily driver. However, the man who picked you up was a temp. I would rather keep things as close to normal for me as possible. If I had used Justin, he would have taken a day off in return, and I can't have that."

"I see, sir. Can we start our discussion you so nicely invited me here for?"

"Well, David, if you don't mind, I would rather rest a bit before we eat, and then I'll recap the life I wrote you about. So if you don't mind, I'll retire for now and see you at the dinner table at five o'clock."

Before David could utter a single word of disappointment, Randolph had risen from his chair and headed toward his room at the base of the stairs in the entryway.

"Damn it, it just seems that he's stringing me along. But why? What is there for him to gain by keeping me here?" David glanced down at his watch to check the time. "Shit, it's only two. Another three fucking hours till dinner, and will it even be worth the wait?" David shook his head from side to side as if to say no. It was more like disbelief. He couldn't fathom staying in his captor's home one more night. At the same time he didn't want to miss a chance to get him back into the game he so loved. "Well, I reckon there is no choice. I've got to stay and take the chance that Randolph really has something worth writing about. If nothing else, it might make for a good human interest story. That alone might get me back to New York, Chicago, or some paper within those leagues."

David turned and walk toward the kitchen. Pushing the swinging door open, he heard, "Mr. Erwin, if that is you, you might as well turn around and leave. There is nothing in here for you or anyone of your kind."

David opened his mouth to speak, but for the first time, he decided it was better not to enrage the sexy Tamara while she was preparing dinner. David turned and went to his room. "How the fuck did that bitch know it was me and not Randolph?" David sat plopped down on his bed and let his head fall back on the pillow.

Looking up at ceiling, staring at the ornate woodwork that adorned the dark, cloudy, crystal light fixture that hung over his bed, David slowly drifted off to sleep.

He awoke in a strange room surrounded by gray smoke. He tried to lift himself, only to find he couldn't move his arms and legs. David looked to his left arm and then his right. To his surprise, there were wide leather straps with large brass buckles latched and locked with old rust-covered medieval-style locks. David opened his mouth to scream, but nothing came out.

"Scream all you like, Mr. Erwin. No one can hear you from down here."

David turned his head in the direction from where the voice was coming from. He saw the sexy Tamara standing there, holding a large knife. Suddenly, David heard, "Wake up, Mr. Erwin. Wake up. It's dinnertime. Mr. Cardigan sent me to retrieve you for dinner."

Dinner? Damn, it was just a dream. David opened his eyes to see Justin walking to the door. "Thanks, Justin. Let me wash the sleep from my eyes and I'll be right there. Thanks."

David entered the dining room to see Tamara serving Randolph. "Just in time, Mr. Erwin. Have a seat. Tamara has made us her fabulous chicken and sausage gumbo. You're in for a real taste sensation."

"I'm sure I am, Randolph. I tried to sneak a peek and maybe an early taste, but she ran me out of the kitchen before I was able to even enter."

"It wasn't the gumbo tasting I was worried about, Mr. Erwin." Tamara placed the silver serving bowl and ladle on the serving cart and stomped off to the kitchen.

"I swear, Randolph. I didn't do anything this time. All I wanted was to sample the gumbo you spoke so highly about."

"Mr. Erwin, you rubbed her raw from the first moment you

stepped into my house with all your glaring looks and sexual comments. You can't expect her to welcome you warmly as if you and you were dear old friends now, can you?"

"I guess not, Randolph. Maybe I need to make it up to her in some way."

"Mr. Erwin, it would be best if you just stayed clear of Tamara entirely. You have already cost me too much money in the raise that I had to give her in order to keep her. I really don't want to have to raise here salary again on account of you. So please, just keep your distance and allow me to keep her here with me for the time that I have left."

"Okay, Randolph. I'll leave her be. But we will need to conclude our business soon. I have to get back to the paper before they give my desk away."

"We will, Mr. Erwin, we will. And I can guarantee your desk is safe and will be there for you when you return. We will start tonight with the recap of my life and the long career I enjoyed. But for now, please sit down and enjoy this superb gumbo."

David pulled out the chair closest to Randolph and sat down. He noticed the vase and the black roses it contained. Thinking it was odd to have black roses on a dinner table, David started to ask Randolph about them but decided against it. He instead opted to dish out some gumbo and rice into his bowl. Randolph picked up the plate containing freshly baked bread, and David took the first piece of bread closest to him on the plate. "Thanks, Randolph." The two men set there quietly, eating the gumbo Tamara had prepared for their dinner. David kept staring at the old dilapidated man sitting to his left, wanting to ask him, "Why the fuck did you bring me here?" But he held his tongue. For David, holding his tongue was never an easy task, but held it he did.

As the two men finished eating, Randolph called for Tamara to have the dishes removed and the table cleared. "Mr. Cardigan, would you care for dessert?"

"No, Tamara. I believe we will just retire to the library for the rest of the evening. Please bring Mr. Erwin and me some tea, and we'll get out of your way."

"Will you be requiring my services any further tonight?"

"No, Tamara. I think Mr. Erwin and I will be busy for the rest of the night and won't need you."

"Then if it is all right with you, I'll finish cleaning up and head into town for a few hours."

"That's fine. Have Justin drive you, and let him know what time you wish to return."

"Thanks, Mr. Cardigan. I will. Good night."

Randolph and David exited the dining room and went into the library. The whole time, David was biting at the bit to ask Randolph what this evening would consist of, but he held back and waited. As the two men sat down, David noticed the books on the end table next to Randolph's chair. One of the books was the same one he saw the day after he arrived at the house of Randolph Cardigan. The title on the spine of the book read *Time for a Serial Killer*. David couldn't make out the title of the other two, but he imagined they had to be the same ones from the day before.

Randolph opened a small wooden box and held it out in front of David. "Care for a smoke, David? They're straight from the tobacco farms in Cuba. They are very mild and full flavored. I believe you will enjoy them."

"Thanks, Randolph. I believe I will." David reached inside the box and pulled out a nice fat cigar. Randolph handed him the cutter and a lighter. David snipped off the end of the cigar and lit it, drawing deeply on the freshly cut end, getting air to flow through it. "Very nice, Randolph. Very nice indeed." David sat back into the chair and puffed on the cigar. As the smoke rose above his eyes, he could see that Randolph had placed three spiral-bound notebooks on the table in front of him.

"Mr. Erwin, these notebooks are for you to write down the information you will need to tell my story."

"So am I to take it we will be starting soon?"

"Yes, Mr. Erwin, we will. I ask that you try not to interrupt me no more than absolutely necessary. I think you will get more from this interview if you listen and take notes than you would from a shit load of questions."

"As you wish, Randolph. I will refrain from the usual question-and-answer interview as you request. I can't promise that I won't ask any questions, but I will try, and we'll see how this goes."

"I can't ask for much more than that, David. Well, I guess the best place to start would be from the so-called beginning or the first killing and how I found myself drawn into this world."

David sat back as Randolph started to talk.

"Well, it was about forty years ago, give or take. I was a traveling salesman going from town to town, showing my wares to every hardware store I came across. That's right, I sold hardware for home repairs and, of course, commercial tools, as well. I was driving through the night so that I could make an eight a.m. appointment in Wytheville, Virginia. It was late, and I was starting to feel the long hours driving weighing heavily on my eyelids."

"So you mean to tell me about true murders you have committed and not some bullshit life story that isn't worth putting pen to paper?"

"Yes, David. What I am about to tell you I have never told a living soul until now. I have been waiting for the right time and the right person to tell the forty years of death that was my life."

"Why me? Why now?"

"David, all will be revealed in time as I tell my story. So if you don't mind, let me take you down this dark path the way I want to so that you understand fully and can best relive it for your readers. Now as I was saying.

"First, I best let you know this was not the first act of atrocity I had committed, but it will be the first one I tell you about. Later we'll get to the first one, but for now you will have to wait for that one.

"Like I said, it was very late, and I was very sleepy. I couldn't afford to stop, not even for a catnap. I had to make my appointment on time. I had been trying to make a sale to this particular store for two months. The owner called and left me a message for me to come by on this day at this time if I even wanted a chance at his business, and I wasn't about to blow it. Just as I crossed the city limits sign entering Wytheville, a deer jumped out in front of my 1964 Impala Super Sport. I swerved to miss it and didn't see what I was about to run into. A young boy had been leaning over to pick something up from the roadside. Just then, the right side of my car impacted with the side of his head. As you can imagine, a car traveling at roughly thirty miles per hour and meeting a human skull would not end well for the owner of that skull.

"As I heard the bumper make contact with the young boy's head, I could hear bone shattering, skin ripping from the skull, and blood spewing upward onto my windshield. I slammed on the brakes, and the car swerved even more, pinning the young head between the right-side fender and the nearby fence post. As the car slowly came to a stop, what seemed to be an eternity, I heard a faint popping sound. I quickly opened the door and stepped out. I stood there for a moment, afraid to walk around to the other side and see what I had done. I was hoping that it was the sleep in my eyes playing tricks on me and it wasn't a boy but a deer that I hit. I walked ever so slowly, almost creeping to the right side of the car. I could see the blood and bits of flesh, bone, and hair in the creases of the bumper where the young head made contact with my once blemish-free car.

"Standing there, looking down at the damage to my car and the evidence of what just happened, I saw something laying on the wet muddy ground slightly in the range of the headlights. It appeared to be something round, but I couldn't make it out. I walked over to where it lay, and in the faint light from the harvest moon I could see it was the head of the young boy I had just hit. That's right. It confirmed my every grimacing nightmare. I had indeed hit a person and not a deer as I had hoped. The faint popping sound I heard was the force of the car swerving, pinning the young head and neck between my car and the fence post, forcing the head free from where it had been permanently attached for the past fourteen years.

"I could only see the outline of the young head with the light from the moon and the one headlight I had left. I went back to the car and reached in the glove compartment for my flashlight. I scrambled around the papers and finally grasped the round cylinder end of the handle. I yanked it free from the compartment and stepped back onto the roadside. I walked over to the where the head lay and pointed the light at it. I had forgotten to turn the damn thing on. I guess maybe I didn't forget. I pushed the switch forward, hoping the batteries were dead. The light beamed out in front of me on to the head as if the sun had come out.

"To my horror. I could see I was right. The young head lay there just in front of me. The vertebra of the neck where it was severed gleamed in the light. Blood oozing from the ripped muscle and skin had jagged bloody edges. I stepped closer to try and see the face or what might be left of it. The impact of the car to the head had all but destroyed it. Anyone else would not have known it was a human head. The face had taken the full force of the impact. All that was left was shattered bits of bone, ripped skin, and peeled back muscle of what once was a young teenage boy. I walked over to the right side of the car, knowing what I would fine but hoping this was all a nightmare that I needed to wake up from.

"There, just on the other side of the barbwire fence, was the lifeless, headless body of the young boy. Laying there with the neck bones protruding from the tissue that once held it tight, the body was dressed in bibbed overalls and a red flannel shirt. His arms lain beside him as if he were asleep in his bed. Unlike a sleeping child, he would never awaken. The clothing he wore gave me the first clue as to who this was. It was the retarded boy that was always walking around, pushing a grocery cart full of tin cans. He spent all his time picking up tin cans to sell at the local scrapyard. Once I had seen him in the hardware store buying penny candy. He stood there for damn near an hour, picking out pieces of peppermint, butterscotch, and lemon drops. Finally, the shop owner had to run him off. I remember asking the owner about him and getting nothing more than 'He's a bother. He always picks through the candy and only buys one or two pieces.'

"What was I to do? Killing the local retard wouldn't go over very good with the local yokels. This would ruin any chance of obtaining the business from the shop owner. I couldn't have this ruin everything. I had worked my ass off for over the past two months. But what, how could I cover this up? I stopped for a second and recalled there was a sinkhole about two miles back. I could drop the head and the body there. No one would ever find it. No one would ever know. I reached down and grabbed both legs of the body and dragged it to the trunk of my car. I opened the back door of the car and reached for the stash of trash bags I keep in the back floorboard. I was always hitting some small animals and used the bags to put them so I could cook them up later if I couldn't find a greasy spoon somewhere.

"I laid the bag out and held open one edge of it and lifted the top of the body where the head used to be attached, and I slid the bag over the shoulders. With the duct tape I carried, I taped the bag to the shoulders. I didn't want it to bleed all over my trunk. That might raise more than a few questions, and I didn't need that. I heaved the heavy corpse up over the edge of the trunk and clasped my hands to the seat of the overhalls and dragged it into the truck. I went back to the head and picked it up and placed it into a bag and into the truck. I slammed the truck closed just in time. I saw car lights in the distance and didn't need anyone to see this.

"A black car pulled alongside of me and the driver stepped out. 'Hey, mister, need any help?' a young voice called from the driver's side. 'No thanks,' I replied. 'I must have run over a nail or something. I'll change my flat and head on into town, but thanks, son.' This explanation satisfied the driver, and he spun off. I walked back to the front of the car to make sure I wasn't leaving anything behind that could tell someone what had taken place on this dreadful night. I took the flashlight from my back pocket, turned it on, and waved it back and forth on the ground. There, just a few feet from where the head had lain, was a small round object. Shit, it was one of the eyes. It had popped out when the head hit the ground. I picked it up and threw it into the woods across the road.

"I got back in my car and turned it around, pointing in the direction of where the sinkhole was. I drove down the road for a few miles and turned off on to a dirt road. Just at the end of the dirt road was the sinkhole. I backed the car up to the edge and opened the trunk. I dragged the body from the trunk onto the soft ground and kicked it over the edge. Then I grabbed the bag holding the mangled head and tossed it into the sinkhole. The hole was so deep that I couldn't hear the sound of the body hitting the bottom. I shined my light down into it to make sure that the body or bag wasn't hung up somewhere.

"I turned my attention to the right side of the car and saw all the damage for the first time. Not only had the impact busted the headlight, but it dented the front edge of the fender. I walked over to get a closer look and could see bits of skin and hair stuck there. I went back to the back seat of my car and got some cleaner and rags and cleaned off the blood, skin, and hair."

"Randolph, you're telling me this killing was nothing more than an accident. Not a murder. I am not sure how this would make you killer."

"Yes, it's true. This one was an accident. But it took me down the road that I would spend my entire life on. Just sit back, take notes, and you'll see what I mean.

"As I was driving back, I couldn't help but recall the feeling that this night had thrust upon me. My heart was still pounding in my chest, my senses were heightened, my mouth was dry, and my hands were clammy. The rush of emotions was unlike anything I had ever known. I couldn't explain it if I tried. I got to town and went to the hotel and checked in. I told the desk clerk that I had to be up no later than seven a.m. He reminded me it was nearly five now and there was little use in going to bed now. I went to the local diner for coffee and a quick bite to eat.

"As I opened the door and looked around the place, it seemed as if everyone was staring at me. My imagination started working overtime. I just about had myself believing everyone knew what I had done. I hung my head and looked at the floor as I walked to a table. Sitting there holding the single sheet of paper that was the menu, the waitress startled me when she asked, 'What you want to drink, sir?' I sat straight up in my seat as if I was shot out of a gun. I ordered coffee with cream and sugar and continued to peer at the menu, looking for something. Not sure what it was, I knew I wasn't hungry, but I couldn't just sit there.

"The waitress returned to my table with the coffee, a small cream pitcher in the shape of a cow, and a bowl of sugar. She was a heavyset older lady, someone's grandma. Her hair was white with touches of auburn mixed in. Her face was weathered and wrinkled, showing she had had a hard life. 'Are you ready to order, sir?'

'I'm not sure. Everything looks so good. What would you recommend?'

'Hum, I never eat here, sir, and wouldn't have a clue about what you might like. So look over the menu and order, if you don't mind. I don't have all day. But stay away from the eggs Benedict. The sauce is nothing but watered-down mayo, and its old.'

'Thanks, ma'am. I'll remember that.'

"She walked off, giving me a few more minutes to think things over, but all I could think about was that poor boy laying at the bottom of the sinkhole. What if someone saw me? What if I missed something? Why was this happening again? Yes, again. It had happened twice before, and both times I got away scot clean."

"Twice, Randolph? What happened twice before? There were two other killings that you haven't told me about?"

"Yes, Mr. Erwin. There were two others. And like I told you in the beginning, you would learn about those in due time. So if you don't mind, I would like to finish this one tonight before I go to bed."

"Of course, Randolph. Please continue."

"I picked up the cow pitcher and tipped it forward, and the cream came pouring out of the mouth of the cow. Suddenly I heard this loud laugh. I turned to see where it had come from, only to find it had come from me. Now the people were looking at me. I laughed again and said, 'It came out the cow's mouth.' The other patrons turned back to their meals and ignored me. That was just what I needed to break the feeling that they had been staring at me.

"The old weathered waitress came back over. 'Ready yet, sir?'

'Yes, ma'am. I'll have the biscuits and gravy with two eggs over easy and an order of bacon.'

'For someone who didn't know what you wanted, you sure did make up your mind fast.'

'Yes, ma'am.' After a bit, she returned with my breakfast. 'Thanks.' I sat there eating and drinking coffee. I was still amused by the cow creamer. The longer I sat, the more at ease I became, realizing that no one was staring at me or knew anything of what went on in the early hours of this morning. I finished eating and went to my meeting. I put out the best presentation of my life and locked in the sale. Hell, the stubborn shop owner wanted me to come by four times a year so he would always be up-to-date on the new products I offered.

"Well, Mr. Erwin, that's enough for tonight. It's late, and I need my rest, so we'll call it a night."

"*Wow*, Randolph. I'll be perfectly honest with you. I was expecting some bullshit old fart reminiscing about past conquests or some crap like that. I didn't expect anything like what you told me tonight."

"Well, David, I hope you've changed your mind and can see what I have to offer you here is much more than just some old fart's stories of meaningless wandering."

"Well, Randolph, for now you have sparked my interest. For that reason alone, I'll stay another night or two to make sure there is something here worth writing. Sorry if that sounds cold, but I can't just write about an accident, no matter how well it was depicted."

"Not at all, David. I wouldn't expect anything less for the perfectionist like you. Good night, David."

Randolph pushed himself up from the chair and walked from the room, disappearing into the hallway as he went to his room. David sat there, scratching his head, wondering if he could have been totally wrong about this. "Hell, if nothing else, I could write a book about an eccentric old man and how he lived his life hiding an accidental murder of a young boy for over forty years. The regrets of a long drive rushing to a meeting caused. Yeah, perfect. I can do something with that alone. A book like this would bring me back to the top, if I am still the writer I once was. What am I saying? I am better than I have ever been. There is no one better than me with words. Only I can do this justice. Only I could tell this the way it needs to be told."

The next morning, David was awakened with the smell of coffee and bacon frying. "Yummy. What a way to wake up." David went to the bathroom and washed the sleep from his face, then headed down to the dining room. Randolph was seated at the table, enjoying his breakfast. "Come on in, David. Breakfast is ready and waiting. Once we are finished, we'll begin again where we left off last night."

David sat down, grabbed a plate, and dished himself up two eggs, three strips of bacon, and poured a cup of coffee. "I've been looking forward to this almost as much as I'm looking forward to hearing more of your stories." After the two men finished eating, they went to the library to continue with Randolph's tales.

"Well, where did I leave off? Oh yeah, I remember. I had just finished with..."

"Randolph, can we start with your first killing? You made

references to two other murders and where they were accidents like the young boy you spoke of. Could we start with those?"

"Like I told you last night, David, we will get to those later. It's not time for them yet. Once I tell you about them, you'll understand why I waited. Trust me and be patient, please. Now back to the next one. Well, it would be two years before the next one would take place, and this time it would not be an accident. After the young boy, I really tried not to think about it. However, from time to time, my mind would go back to that fateful night and replay the events over in my head. Wondering what if, what if there hadn't been any fog? What if I had stopped earlier like I wanted to? What if I drove slower like I normally did? Just a shit ton of what ifs. No matter how I worked it in my head, the results were the same. The boy was still dead. The main issue wasn't the death of the boy. It was the feeling I kept getting when I thought about his death. The feeling of empowerment, holding someone's life in my hands, being in control of whether he'd live or die. That's one feeling I was never able to shake. The more I thought about it, the more I wanted to have that feeling again and again. I came to the conclusion I would never be able to feel like that unless I killed someone again.

"That day I decided I would never kill again. I would never feel the control over life or death again. So I put those thoughts into the deepest recesses of my mind. Back into the darkest area of my subconscious, never to surface or haunt my thoughts. Held there, I was certain they wouldn't show their ugly faces. I couldn't have been more wrong.

"I was on my quarterly visit to the hardware shop in the town where the boy lived. I had not thought of that fateful night in more than six months. I had not been bothered with those dark thoughts since I placed them into cemeteries in my mind. Walking into the shop, I was met by a beautiful set of green eyes. Never had a pair of eyes pierced a soul as deep as those glowing mint green eyes. I had not even noticed the form of the body they belonged to. Once I had overcome the whirlwind of shock those eyes sent me into, I focused on the woman in front of me, asking if she could help me.

'I'm sorry, ma'am. I am Randolph Cardigan, this area's regional salesman for Blackhawk Tools. I am on my quarterly visit to the area. Is Mr. Goodwin in?'

'Yes, my husband is in the back. Let me go get him.'

"As she walked away, her ass swung from side to side. My eyes couldn't stop watching it sway. It was like the movement of a fine handmade Rolex watch. Nothing could move as sweetly or as effortlessly as that ass. Oh, to hold that ass in my hands. Could something sexual be heaven on earth? Could this goddess with the glowing mint green eyes give herself to me for hours of maddening lustful sex? The kind of sex only known by very few men on earth, the type of encounter I had never known.

'Mr. Cardigan, it is nice to see you again. What new items have you brought with you this time for me to offer my customers?'

'Nice to see you again, Mr. Goodwin. I've brought several new types of hammers, the new circular saw, and a few other items I am certain your customers will love.'

'Wonderful, Mr. Cardigan. Would it be possible for you to come back tonight right before closing time so I can have the time to look everything over and decide what type of order I'll be placing?'

'Sure, Mr. Goodwin, but I must ask you to call me Randolph, please. And I'll come back around five o'clock and we'll take all the time we need.'

'Thank you. I'll see you then. Faith, would you show Randolph out?'

'Sure. Why not, I do nothing else around here. I could at least walk some damn salesman to the door. I have nothing better to do. This way, salesman. Just follow me.'

"She turned and walked toward the door, and the swing of that perfect ass caught my eyes again. I was afraid that Mr. Goodwin would see me leering at his wife's ass. I did my best to hold back and keep my eyes from giving me away. But that ass, that perfect ass—I had to have that ass. Was it the ass? Was it those glowing mint green eyes? I wasn't totally sure what held me captivated by this woman. All I knew was I would do anything to possess her for the briefest of time. Behold her magnificent natural body. To see that ass without the cover of clothing. Anything, everything, and what wouldn't I do to have her.

"As I was leaving, I stopped at the door to ask Faith where a good restaurant was. 'Faith, I'm sorry if I have intruded on something here. I can come back another time if it would be more convenient.'

'No, Mr. Cardigan, there is no convenient time. Come back when you told Dan you would and make your pitch to him. I am sure the folks around here will want whatever you're selling, no matter how stupid it may be. Tools and more tools—that is all Dan cares about.'

'Again let me apologize for the intrusion. It would seem I've come at a bad time.'

'Like I said, there is no good time. It wouldn't matter when you come. You have a job to do, and you have a living to earn, so come back at five.'

'Thanks, ma'am, but could I ask one more thing? Where would you recommend me to grab a nice lunch at?'

'Well, there is the small café just down the street. It's nice. The food isn't bad, but it's nothing special. If it was dinner and you were asking me out, I would take me to the new French bistro in Roanoke. But no one ever asks me out anymore. Not since last month when I messed up and married Dan. Yeah, the café would be your best choice for lunch, Mr. Cardigan.'

'Would Mr. Goodwin be all right with me offering to buy you lunch? I could use the company.'

'I don't really care if he does or don't. I go where I please.'

'Well, in that case, would join me for lunch?'

'Sure, and I can show you where the café is, and Dan can go get fucked.' I was very surprised to hear her talk the way she did about her husband. It told me how strained the new marriage was. This could be all I needed to obtain that perfect ass and watch those eyes glow even more than they already were.

"We walked out and went down the street to the small country café. It was the same place I had eaten at the morning after the young boy died. As we were walking down the street, Faith was still rambling about how she thought it would be different. All I could think of was if that same old woman was still working there and the early morning prior to me stopping in and having breakfast. The thoughts and feelings I thought I had buried all of a sudden came flooding over me. How I missed that feeling. I tried hard to push it back into the hidden area where it had lain dormant these many months. Nothing I was doing would bury these feelings, not even the sounds of Faith's rambling. If she had asked, I wouldn't have been able to tell her two things she was going on about.

"We arrived at the diner and sat down. The same old woman came up and took our order. 'Mr. Cardigan.'

'Please, call me Randolph. Mr. anything sounds so formal.'

'Okay, Randolph, can I ask you something?'

'Sure, you may ask me anything you wish.'

'Am I an attractive woman? I mean, do you find me desirable? If I wasn't married, that is.'

'Faith, my I call you Faith?'

'Sure.'

'Faith, any man would count himself lucky just to be in the same room with you. If you weren't married to one of my best clients, I would ask you out in a heartbeat. I would take you to the city and show you the time of your life.'

'Would you now? Dan always seemed to find me attractive, but since we tied the knot, he just seems to treat me like an employee. Hell, come to think of it, he has always treated me that way. Even when I was working for him and fucking him, he still treated me that way. If I hadn't gotten knocked up, he would have kept screwing me and never would have tied the knot.'

'You used to work for Dan? How come I never saw you there before now?'

'Well, I used to help him in the mornings and on the nights he needed to do inventory. But inventory was getting to be every other night. Then it was just screwing. We never got around to that damn inventory.'

'I see. I would not have guessed you were pregnant.'

'Oh, I'm not. It was a false alarm, and I guess Dan thinks it was some sort of trap to getting him to marry me. But it wasn't. I really thought I was knocked up. Everything was pointing to that. It was three weeks after the wedding when I got my period and found out it was a false alarm. Dan bitched for a month about that, and nothing I could say to him would get him to believe any different.'

'Well, if it is any consolation, you're one of the most attractive pregnant women I know.'

'Thank you, Randolph. I needed to hear that from someone.'

'Well, I guess we better eat and let you get on back to the store. I have to go down to the motel and see if they have any rooms available for the night. If they do, then I reckon I'll take me a nap to kill some time until five.'

'You're going to be staying the night? That's nice. Maybe I'll see in the morning here before you leave out. I come here for breakfast almost every day. They have the best biscuits and gravy. Will you be staying at the hotel just down the street or the motel just outside of town?'

'I guess the one down the street. It's closer, and I won't have to drive back into town for my meeting.'

'Yeah, it's a nicer place too.'

"We finished eating lunch and kept talking. The more she talked about Dan, the more I knew I would have that sweet ass before I left. We walked out of the diner and she said goodbye. As she walked off, I kept staring at that amazing ass and couldn't get those eyes out of my mind. I would find a way to get into those pants before I left. I walked down to the hotel and grabbed a room for my afternoon nap and told the desk clerk to ring my room around four thirty so I wouldn't be late for my meeting.

"I awoke to a knock on the door of my room. I glanced down at my watch for the time and saw it was four thirty. I yelled in the direction of the door, 'I'm awake. Thanks.' However, the knocking persisted. I walked over and opened the door. To my astonishment, I was met by those same haunting, glowing mint green eyes. 'Ms. Goodwin, what can I do for you?'

'Dan was afraid that the hotel might let you oversleep, so he asked me to come and make sure you would make the meeting on time.'

'I see. That was very considerate of Dan and mighty nice of you to do so. Thanks so very much. I am sure the desk clerk would have missed waking me up, seeing what time it is now.'

'No, he was on his way up here when I got the desk and asked for your room number. Also, I had my own motive by coming over here.'

'And what might that be, Faith?'

'Well, I asked Dan to take me to the new French bistro in Roanoke tonight and he said hell no. He was too busy and had to complete the weekly inventory. You see, he hired a new girl two weeks ago, and the whole inventory shit started up again within a few days. I told that blond bitch to leave Dan alone and find another job, but she won't. I think I'm going to have to whoop her ass.'

'I'm sorry to hear that, Faith. But it doesn't explain your motive for coming over.'

'No, I guess it don't. I was wondering if you have ever eaten there.'

'No, I don't go to many places once I get home. I am rather a homebody.'

'I see. I sure would love to go there. It would mean the world to me.'

"I stood there for a few seconds, mulling the thought over on my head. Should I ask her? I'm certain she would say yes. That would definitely give me the chance I need to climb up that skirt of hers. 'Well, Faith, I'd be more than happy to take you there tonight if you think Dan wouldn't be upset with me taking you.'

'Hell no. If it is the same inventory me and him use to do, he'll be there till one or two in the morning. And if not, fuck him. If he doesn't want me to enjoy a night out at a fine restaurant with him, then I'll find someone who will.'

'Well, if you're sure, then I would be happy to take you out for some fine food. Everyone needs to experience the finer things in life at least once. Our meeting usually lasts about an hour, maybe a little more. I'll meet you back here once we have concluded our business, and we'll be off.'

'I can't meet you here. Everyone in town will be talking about that by morning if I did. As you're leaving town heading toward Roanoke, there's a small road that turns off to the right. Go down that road until you come to a grove of trees. Just as your car gets into them there, I'll be waiting.'

'That will be great. I'll come straight there after my meeting with Dan.'

"We left the hotel and walked over to the store. Mr. Goodwin was waiting there behind the counter as we walked in. 'Hi, Randolph. Thanks for waiting till the day's business was done for your sales pitch.'

'Not a problem, Mr. Goodwin. I am only too happy to arrange my schedule to meet the needs of my clients. And thank you for sending your lovely wife over to make sure I didn't oversleep and keep you waiting. That was very nice of both of you.'

'Randolph, please call me Dan. If you call me Dan, I won't call you Mr. Cardigan.'

'That's a deal, Dan. Let me get a few things out of the car and we'll get down to business.' I walked out and came back in with two cases. As we started to talk, Faith excused herself and left. Dan and I got down to business. I showed him a few items and he placed his usual order, plus some of the new items I had shown him. I left around six thirty to go meet up with Faith.

"I went back to the hotel and checked out. The deck clerk asked me why I was leaving so soon. I told him I had finished my business and had plenty of time to get home before it was too late. As I drove out of town, I was planning everything over in my head. I would take her to dinner, and when I brought her back, I would have my way with her. At no time did killing her even cross my mind. I wanted to carry on some sort of affair where when I came through town, I would be able to get that ass when I wanted to. I turned down the small road and drove past the trees. There she was, waiting, just like she said she would be. She was dressed to kill. She was wearing a blue tight-fitting dress that came down to her knees, a black belt, and a white sweater. You could have knocked me out with a feather. She looked so fantastic I wanted to bend her over the hood and take her right then. But I held back. I didn't want to run her off and lose what might be the only shot I would get.

'Hi, Faith. Should we take your car or mine?'

'Well, I think it would be best that we took your car. I told Dan I was going to my mother's in Bristol and would be back late.'

'That's great. So we can take our time and really enjoy the meal.'

'Yes, we can.' She got in my car, and we started driving north toward Roanoke. She talked my ear off the whole way. We finally got to the restaurant she wanted so badly to go to. It wasn't until we were on our way back when the thoughts of killing started seeping in. At first it was just passing thoughts, and I shook them off as quickly as they entered my mind. The more she talked, the more often they popped up. I could tell she was a money-hungry, gold-digging bitch. She continuously talked about how she had to ask Dan for money to do this or that and how big of a tightwad he was. She even made a reference to how things would be so much better if she left him, but then she wouldn't get one dime.

"When we got back to her car, I started making my moves. At first ever so slightly. I finally leaned over once I was sure I would have her and kissed her.

'Mr. Randolph, I never expected that.' 'Was it too soon? I had wanted to do that since I picked you up.'

'No, not at all. I had been hoping you would do something like that before now. But hey, now is fine too.'

It was a beautiful night, so I suggested we step out of the car and continue this. She opened her door and I mine. We both stepped to the back. 'I'll get a blanket out so you will be more comfortable.'

'Aw, that is so sweet. You don't want me to get my ass dirty. What a true gentleman.'

"I opened the trunk, and there staring me in the face was one of the new missionary hammers I had shown Dan earlier that day. One end square and blunt with ridges. The other end was long and flat, more like a wedge. It was used for breaking bricks into smaller sizes for corners of walls.

"As I was picking up the blanket, those thoughts came rushing in. It would be so easy. No one was around for mile to hear her screams. But what would I do with the body? I turned around with blanket in hand when I was met by those wonderful glowing eyes. In the dark of the night with a full moon shining down, her golden hair reflected the light of the moon like morning dew on a spider's web in the early morning sun. Our eyes met, and she smiled brightly with the edges of her cute thin mouth curling upward toward the high hung moon.

"She eased in closer and softly pressed her lips to mine. Nothing sweeter had I tasted in all my days. As we were locked in our longing embrace, she moved her right hand down my chest, over my stomach, loosened my belt, and undid the button on my pants. As she reached inside, a wondrous feeling came sweeping over me like the cool crisp water falling over a mountain waterfall. There was no chance in stopping her next actions as she dropped to her knees and began to pleasure me in a way that I had never known. All of a sudden, those thoughts started filling my head. The harder she worked at pleasing me, the stronger the feeling got. I laid my hand on the back of her head and gripped her golden hair and pulled slightly. My other hand was in the trunk, holding me up, and I could feel the wooden handle of one of the missionary hammers I had shown Dan earlier in the day.

"The wooden handle under my hand was the encouragement I needed. The handle filled my hand as my fingers wrapped around the oval-shaped handle. The feeling of the wood meeting flesh was almost too much to hold back. My fingers caressed the hammer slowly at first, slipping up and down the handle as she performed the amazing act of pleasure. As the pleasure intensified, the faster I stroked the handle. Suddenly the hammer was rising from the carpet-covered floor of my trunk. Higher and higher it climbed. The closer I got to sexual fulfillment, the higher the hammer climbed, until my arm was fully extended. The silver metal of the hammerhead shimmered in the light of the moon. The moonlight danced along the edges of the long wedge side and caught my eyes. Right as I reached the maximum depths of pleasure, the hammer seemed to have a mind of its own and started turning in the direction of the precious angel giving me pleasure. I could not contain the emotion welling inside me. She turned her eyes upward toward mine as if to make sure she was doing things right and I was getting the maximum amount of pleasure she could possibly give to me.

"Without warning, and with the swiftness of lightning, the hammer fell downward. She never saw it coming. She couldn't even imagine the end she had planned for me wasn't the end I had in mind. As I reached my climax, the wedge end of the hammer reached its new home as well. With her eyes focused on mine and her movements now stopped, I could see signs of wetness dripping down her forehead in the red glow of my taillights. The wetness at first looked as if it was sweat, but you and I know what it really was. She fell limp at my feet, and I moved to the side. With the white glow of the taillight, I could now see the full impact of the hammer. It happened so fast I almost missed.

"There she lay on ground behind my car, and only one thought came to me. I couldn't help but think how little amount of blood there was. I would have bet there would have been much more than that. I buttoned and zipped my pants, a double explosion of pleasure. Once with the climax of pleasure Faith brought me to, and the other when the hammer entered skull and separated her life from her body. I walked around the car and sat down in the front seat to enjoy the moment. The light bounced off the rearview mirror and caught my attention. I looked up to see my face for the first time. There looking back at me wasn't the face I woke to that morning. Now it was covered with the still wet blood that had shot out and up from the impact of the hammer with Faith's skull. I hadn't realized her blood had sprayed up into my face. But right there in the center of my forehead was a small lump—red and wet from the still fresh blood from Faith. I grabbed a rag from the back seat to wipe the evidence from my face. At first, I wasn't sure what it could be. Maybe something that was stuck to the hammer that had flew off while it swung it. No, hell no, it couldn't be. The impact couldn't have been that hard. Not hard enough to tear chunks of gray matter. Brain. It was her brain. Right there, stuck in the middle of my forehead. A small piece of the muscle that held the personality, emotions, faults, and everything that was Faith, right there on my forehead.

"Once I overcame the shock of finding Faith's brain stuck on my head, I was faced with the fact that I had just purposely killed someone. Sure, I had killed before, but before it was an accident. This time it was me. It was by my hand and not some freak accident. I had taken someone's life. Not just someone. It was Faith, Dan's wife. She was still lying there behind my car. What was I going to do with her body? There was the sinkhole. But her car...what about that? The sinkhole would hide her body. That wasn't an issue. The car, on the other hand, I wasn't sure if it fit. I had to hide both at the same time. But how? Where? I remembered how winding the road was and narrow in some parts. Maybe driving it over the edge. Nah, that wouldn't work. Someone would find it at the bottom. Then they would find she hadn't died in the crash, and then they would be looking for a killer, looking for me.

"I sat there for what seemed like hours before I decided to put her body behind the wheel of her car and tow her and it up to the top of the mountain. Once there, I would set it up to where it would take the slightest push to send it over the edge. I grabbed a small piece of rope from my back seat where Dan had left it. What luck. I wouldn't have to search for anything to act as a wick to ignite the gas in the tank. I lit my makeshift fuse, waited a few seconds, and gave it the nudge it needed to send it spiraling end over end. Two or three flips were all it would need prior to bursting into flames, and the tank exploded. It must have been closer than I thought because the explosion knocked me back. I stepped back to the edge so I could get a better view. Flashes of red, orange, blue, and yellow lit up the night. Just then, I thought I had better get the hell out of there. Someone must have heard the explosion and would be coming soon. If I were lucky enough, I would be able to get off the mountain without anyone seeing my car. I headed back to Roanoke. As I reached the bottom, I could see the faint glow of headlights topping the hillside. Just in time. Yeah, I got out of there just in time. Well, that was the first real murder that I committed. Tomorrow will come the next one. Right now I am tired and need my rest."

"Randolph, you really killed that woman? Is that what you're telling me?"

"That's what I told you. Did you think I was bullshitting you? That all this would be some old fuck rambling on and making shit up? When you leave here, you'll have all the information you need to verify every killing."

"Okay. And if everything checks out, I'll write every word and make sure it is published for everyone to read. I have many questions that you haven't answered yet. When can I expect the answers to these questions?"

"As I told you, you will have all the information before you leave here. Not everything has to be told in the order of which it happened. For now, I bid you goodnight; and we'll start up again after lunch. I have a few things I need to take care of before we can."

"That's fine. I'll talk to you then. Goodnight for now."

David excused himself and went to his room. He was not sure whether he could believe what Randolph told him or not. Sitting there alone in his room, he heard the faint sounds of a woman's footsteps coming down the hall. "Aw, sweet Tamara." David listened for her footsteps to pass by his room. Then he could crack the door and get a nice, well-deserved look at Tamara's sweet, chiseled. rounded ass. David couldn't keep his thoughts on what he was there for or, more to the point, of how he would get out of there. Just then, the steps stopped right outside David's door. He sat there looking at the door, hoping she would twist the handle and invite herself in for a nightcap. At least the type of nightcap David had been dreaming about. The more David stared at the handle on the door, the more he thought he could see it start to turn. The anticipation of waiting was almost too much for David, when suddenly the handle was turning and the door was opening slowly. It was just a small crack at first, as if someone was listening to see if anyone would invite them in.

David opened his mouth to say something when the door swung open. Standing there was Justin. "Mr. Erwin, would you come with me? Mr. Cardigan wanted me to take you into town so you could get some clean clothes and anything else you might need."

"Justin, that would be great. I've been in these duds since I got here."

"There are some rules you must agree to before we can go anywhere."

"All right, I guess I really don't have a choice in the matter if I want clean duds."

"No, sir, you really do not. First, you will be blindfolded as before. I am only allowed to take you to your home, and you must remain within sight at all times. There will be no other stops made, not even to the paper. Is all this understood, Mr. Erwin?"

"Yes, Justin, I expected nothing less. Hell, at least I will be able to change my dirty underwear."

Justin held open the back door of the black car with the blacked-out windows for David to enter. Right before David entered the car, Justin put the blindfold over David's eyes to ensure he would not be able to see how to get back to the house once he would be able to leave.

The car took the same path back to town as it had to get to Mr. Cardigan's house. David remembered some of the same curves and the time frame in which it took them to get to the house from his office. After driving around for a while, the car came to a stop. "Mr. Erwin, we are here. Once again, I must remind you not to talk to anyone. We know you do not associate with any of your neighbors, and they can't stand you either. So please don't try anything stupid."

"Justin, I will be on my best behavior. All I want is a quick shower and change clothes."

"No shower. Just grab what you need so we can go."

"Fine. I'll get my stuff and we can be on our way."

Justin followed David up the steps to the front door of the old French-style home. Old black wrought iron banisters adorned the upper deck while the front porch had nice white fluted columns. As they reached the porch, Justin commented on the need for the house to be painted. He could see the white paint flaking away from the grooves in the fluted columns. "Mr. Erwin, you really might want to get someone to come and paint this place to bring it back to life as it was when it was built."

"Well, Justin, I wasn't really worried too much about it before now. I was hoping to be moving back to New York or Chicago one day."

"Yeah, but in the meantime, why not bring it back to life and increase its value for when you decide to sell it and move on?"

"You got a point there. I will take care of that when Mr. Cardigan and I have completed our business."

David went right to his bedroom closet and took out a small brown leather overnight bag. Justin hung with David's every move. When David went over to his nightstand, Justin seamed to get a bit nervous. David reached for the knob on the drawer and slowly pulled it out. He reached in and heard, "Mr. Erwin, you will not find what you're looking for in that drawer. See, Mr. Cardigan and I already moved the gun to a safer place. So please get what you need and let's get back to the house."

"Sure thing, Justin." David stuffed a few meager clothes into his overnight bag and looked at Justin. The two men went back to the car. Before Justin blindfolded David again, David asked, "If you came over here and removed my gun, why didn't you just get my things for me?"

"Well, Mr. Erwin, Mr. Cardigan wanted you to know that he knew everything about you. Right down to those black-and-white striped boxers you packed into your bag. Now let's be on our way, sir."

For the entire ride back to the house, David couldn't figure out how they knew where he kept his gun. *Wait a second, my black-and-white striped boxers. How the hell could they know I grabbed those exact boxers? Did they place some sort of camera in his home?* He didn't see anything that would have indicated a closed-circuit camera.

Nothing seemed out of place. But how else could he explain this? "Justin, tell me how you knew I had grabbed those black-and-white striped boxers."

"Mr. Erwin, I cannot tell you something I don't know. Mr. Cardigan told me before I came upstairs to get you, what you would do, and what you would place in your overnight bag. Beyond that, I have no clue. I learned a long time ago not to ask or question Mr. Cardigan when he came up with off-the-wall shit like that."

"Mr. Cardigan told you before we ever left the house."

"Yes, sir. So I suspect if you really want to know the answer to that, you will need to ask Mr. Cardigan. However, I doubt if you will get any answers until he is ready to tell you."

The car pulled up to the house and again David was allowed to see. David climbed those same dilapidated steps to the front door. David turned to ask Justin something else, only to see the black car speed off just like it did the first night it brought him there. David shrugged and went into the house. He walked as fast as he could to the library and slung open the door. "Randolph! Damn it, he ain't here." The door suddenly closed, and David turned to find Tamara standing in front of it.

"Mr. Erwin, the way you entered this room, it is clear you are upset. Is there something I can do to ensure that you stay that way?"

"No, you do that already. But you can tell me where Randolph is. I have a bone to pick with him."

"Well, he retired for the evening and asked that he not be disturbed. So unless it is a matter of life or death, I suggest it wait till tomorrow."

"Well, I reckon I'll have to wait for some answers."

"What kind of answers are you looking for, Mr. Erwin?"

"I think Randolph has been watching me for some time now,

and I want to know why. There are just too many things that haven't added up. Like how he had Justin remove my gun from my nightstand and what clothes I had put in my overnight bag. He had to be watching me. That's the only answer that makes sense, and I want to know why and for how long."

"Well, Mr. Erwin, I could tell you, but you wouldn't believe me, so I'll just shut my mouth."

"Tamara, if you know something, I would appreciate you letting me know. So I will ask you something I never ask women and ask you to open your mouth and explain it to me."

"Well, with such an eloquent way to ask me, I'll have to say fuck off and find out on your own. Good night, Mr. Erwin, and good luck on getting your answers."

Tamara turned and slammed the door behind her. The sound of the door slamming against the hard wooden surface of the doorjamb echoed through the house like shockwaves through water. David reached up and stuck his figure in his ear to try to clear the ringing left behind by the slamming door. "That bitch is getting on my nerves. She really needs to get laid. All I asked for was some damn information. Is that too damn much to ask for?" David went into the bathroom and got ready for bed. Just then he heard the door to his room open again. "Damn it, Tamara, if you're just going to be a first-class bitch when I ask you a question, then just leave and I'll find them out the hard way." He turned and walked back into his room to find the door wide open and no one there. David walked over to the door, grabbed the handle, and started to close it and stuck his head out into the hallway. "What the fuck. The least you could've done was close the damn door." The door slammed shut behind him as he walked over to his bed and climbed under the covers. It wasn't long before David was fast asleep.

The next morning, David woke to that all too familiar smell of bacon and eggs frying. "Ah, a quick shower and then breakfast and coffee." He hurried up and jumped into the shower and lathered up. The more he lathered himself up, the more he found himself fantasizing about Tamara. First he pictured her in a cute little maid's outfit, then dressed up as a high school cheerleader, bouncing back and forth from one fantasy to another until he had was finally satisfied.

"Damn, I have to think of more ways to picture her. Those are starting to get old."

David finished getting dressed and went downstairs for breakfast. He entered the dining room all ready to start hammering on Randolph about him spying on him, only to find the room empty, just a few plates on the table and the floral centerpiece. He sat down at the table and waited for a few minutes for Tamara to come in with the food and coffee.

After what seemed like fifteen minutes or so, David got up and walked to the kitchen. "Tamara, I have been waiting in the dining room for you to bring out breakfast for a while."

"Mr. Erwin, I only serve in there when Mr. Cardigan will be eating. This morning, he had to go into town and ate earlier."

"But I could have sworn I smelled the usual. That's why I ran down here so fast so I wouldn't miss it and have to bother you."

"Bother me indeed. Like you give a flying shit if you bother me. Go have a seat and I'll bring you your coffee and food like the maid you dream I am."

David went back into the dining room and sat back down. The whole time he was thinking to himself, *What is with these people? They seem to know what I'm thinking, dreaming. Damn it, they're even getting into my sex fantasies. I just don't get it.* Tamara rolled the cart containing a pot of coffee and sugar. "What, no food?"

"Hold your horses, Mr. Erwin. I do have to cook the food before bringing it out. Unless you would rather I just put raw bacon and eggs on a plate and serve it to you like that. If not, I suggest you don't get your panties in a bunch and wait." She went back to the kitchen to prepare David's morning meal "Mr. Erwin, you need to remember that I work for Mr. Cardigan and not for you."

David scratched his head, poured himself a cup of coffee, and waited for Tamara to bring in the food. "I hope you are frying the bacon crispy and the eggs over easy." A sound of pans clanging rang out of the kitchen and David knew he had hit that nerve of Tamara's. "Did I say something wrong?" he asked, knowing it would push Tamara's buttons even more.

Tamara walked into the dining room and dropped the plate on the table in front of David. "Say something wrong! Mr. Erwin, you've been saying something wrong ever since you came here. For the life of me, I don't know why Mr. Cardigan wants you here in the first place. Maybe it's some sort of atonement he is trying to pay off before he dies. I just don't understand why he needs you here so badly."

"Well, Tamara, he has a story to tell and wants me to write about it. That's the only reason I'm here."

"Well, Mr. Erwin, I wish you would get it done and leave. Mr. Cardigan is a very sweet man and doesn't have much time left. He has cancer, and his doctor has given him six months to live. That was four months ago. I really don't want his last days to be filled with a piece of shit pig like you drooling over his life's story."

"Well, if you feel that strongly about me being here, why don't you tell Randolph?"

"Oh, I have. I have many times, and Mr. Cardigan tells me that he needs you here each and every day until he dies. Why can't you just leave and let him be? What kind of story could be this important to you that you can't let a man die in peace?"

"Tamara, you don't understand. I don't want to be here. I have no choice. Randolph won't let me leave. He's watching my every move. Hell, he told Justin the color of my damn underwear before I even left the house last night. Now tell me how in the fuck he knew what color they would be even before I knew. Tell me that, Tamara."

"Mr. Erwin, that's easy. Mr. Cardigan is psychic. He knows things. He told me just this morning that if I wanted to shock you, I should just make a comment about me being the maid you fantasize about in the shower."

"See, that's what I'm talking about. How in the hell does he know what I daydream about? Psychic my Aunt Fanny. He's no more psychic than I am, and there is nothing you can say to get me to buy into that bullshit."

"Mr. Erwin, you can believe what you want. I really don't care. As for me, Mr. Cardigan has told me too many things for me not to believe he has some sort of psychic powers. It's that or voodoo, and I don't see he him messing around with that shit."

"Either case, I don't get it. But I do thank you for giving me some insight, even if I think it's crap. At least you told me what you believe, and that's a start. Thanks, Tamara."

"Mr. Erwin, believe as you will, I know. The night you arrived here at the house, Mr. Cardigan told me that you would be watching my ass like it was a sports game. He went as far as to tell me what I would say, almost every word. Nobody can just guess at that kind of shit."

"Yeah, I see what you're saying. But how the hell does he know this shit? What really bugs me is what else he knows about me and why he gives a damn."

"Well, Mr. Erwin, I don't know what he might know about you. All I do know is he has some sort of powers that are beyond my knowledge. I don't even question it anymore, and I suggest you do the same."

"Tamara, did it really bother you that I was looking at your ass? Or was it the fact that Randolph told you I would be watching you?"

"Well, I know men look and stare at a woman's backside, and that, in itself, has never bothered me. However, when Mr. Cardigan told me what you would be doing and how I would act, it was almost like I couldn't keep from saying the things I did or act like a bitch. It could have been where Mr. Cardigan told me about it, or it might be that I was just sick and tired of men drooling after me like a steak on a platter. I don't really know. Maybe if he hadn't said anything, I might not have acted in that manner. Who knows. What is done is done."

"I know. Sometimes when we know things, we act very different than if we never knew. Thanks for sitting here and answering these questions of mine, even though it brought up more question than answers."

"Mr. Erwin, just leave your dishes here when you're done and I will come back and get them later. I have a few things I need to finish up before I go to town for the week's shopping."

"Again, Tamara, thanks. And if there is anything I can do to help, let me know. I'm going to be quite bored until Randolph returns. Has he gone to the doctor again?"

"No, he said he had some things he needed to put in order before he dies. I keep asking him not to talk like that, but he seems to think he will be dead by the end of the week."

"I didn't know he was that sick."

"His doctor has told me he could live for another five or six years. That is if he keeps his treatment up and the cancer stays in remission."

"Remission? His cancer is in remission? He lets on like he is still dying from the cancer, and you're telling me it's in remission. Part of the reason I am still here was because he was dying. What a fucking joke! He uses the cancer as a pity factor to get people to feel sorry for him."

"Mr. Cardigan doesn't use his illness for that reason. I don't know how you got that from what I've told, but he isn't like that at all. He doesn't want anyone to feel sorry for him. He would rather no one knew about it at all. I bet if you asked him how he was doing health wise, he would tell you the truth. Then he would tell you he will die this week."

"If he isn't trying to use his illness for a pity trip, then why does he think he will die this week?"

"I do not know. He just feels that he will die this week. He has even pinpointed it down to the day. He says Saturday will be his last day on earth. He has even told me that he wanted his last meal to be my Swedish meatballs. He wants me to serve it for lunch. That leads me to believe he thinks he won't live to see dinner. Well, Mr. Erwin, I have to get back to work. If you would like, we can continue this later after you and Mr. Cardigan have finished for the evening. Just let me know."

Tamara walked out of the dining room toward the main hall and left the door open behind her. This struck David as odd, seeing how she usually slammed doors when he was present. He finished eating his breakfast and sat there for a while, thinking. He was thinking about everything Tamara had told him, about the cancer thing, and about everything else. "I just don't get it. If he isn't dying from cancer, why would he think he will die on Saturday? It doesn't make sense. Randolph doesn't strike me as the superstitious type.

Did some bayou voodoo bitch fill his head full of shit and now he can't shake it? Oh well, it doesn't matter. I'll go along with it for now and listen to his stories. Maybe I'll get lucky and I can write a fiction book with this crap." In David's mind, he had a new plan—a plan that might just make him some money and get him out of the hellhole of the paper he has been condemned to.

On the way back to his room, David heard Tamara singing in her room. She was singing some Cajun song he had never heard. A sneaking image started creeping into his head. An image of an old bayou woman in one of those New Orleans voodoo shops, singing and trying to sell her voodoo shit. Could Tamara be one of those voodoo priestesses? Could she be the reason Randolph thinks he will die on Saturday? She just didn't seem to be the type. She didn't seem to fit the typical stereotype of a voodoo priestess. Maybe it was nothing more than David's imagination running wild. Maybe it was him thinking about Randolph that put that thought in his head. Whatever it was, David wouldn't let himself believe Tamara was one of those people who put hexes on people. "Nah, she ain't one of them. She just likes that zydeco music. That's all it is."

He walked up to Tamara's room in hopes of getting a glimpse of that gorgeous ass, maybe even bare. *Oh yeah, her bare ass would be so sweet to see.* David walked up to the slightly open door and peeked inside. At first he couldn't see anything, and then it happened. Tamara walked past her door. David thought he was seeing things at first. The light and his imagination were playing a trick on him. But then there she was again, with nothing on her beautiful body but a smile. She was still humming that song, but David no longer heard that. He was too fixated on Tamara's smooth warmly tanned body. The type of body that drove men to war in order to possess it, to possess her. Men have gone to war for women of lesser quality. David could see himself possessing that body for a short time; however, no one would be able to possess her for very long.

He was lost in his daydreams, standing there at her door, wishing she would walk slowly over to the door, open it, and invite him in. In his dreams, she would do more than invite him in. She would swing the door open, hard enough to rip it clean off its hinges. She would take David by the hand, lead him into the room, throw him on the bed, and slowly take his clothes off. She would take her time in getting them off him. It would be sheer torture—the type of torture he could only dream of. Slow, relentless torture. David snapped back to reality when the door suddenly swung open. For a second, David thought his daydream would come true.

"Mr. Erwin! What the hell are you doing lurking outside my door? Never mind, I see what you were doing. Give me a damn break. For a second downstairs, I thought we might have made a breakthrough. That you might have not been the pig I thought you were. But here I find you peeking in through my door. I hope you got a damn good look 'cause it's all you'll ever get. I hope what you saw will add spice to those wet dreams you've been having. Now you really have something to visualize about in the shower. Now if you don't mind, get the fuck away from my door and leave me the hell alone."

The door slammed sharply in David's face. As he turned to walk away, he heard Tamara muttering something behind the thick wooden door. He pressed his ear hard against the wooden surface so he could hear better. "Damn it, he spoiled everything. Just when I was getting ready to offer myself to him, he had to go and spoil it." Sniff, sniff. "Now there is no way I can allow myself to feel these feelings for him. He just had to be a fucking pig."

David walked back to his room, wishing he hadn't gone to the open door, wishing he hadn't looked to see what was beyond it, regretting the last fifteen minutes of his life that destroyed any chance he had of tapping that sweet ass. "Are you kidding me? She has fallen for me. But how can I turn this around and make it seem like I'm not the man she's certain I am? What can I do to change this? What can I do to change her mind about me?" David lay back on his bed to ponder his new problem. How would he be able to correct this mess he caused for himself?

David fell asleep with the soft thoughts of Tamara running through his mind. His dreams took him further and closer to Tamara than he could hope for. In his dreams, he would enjoy the soft kisses, warm touch, and tender embrace from a woman he could do nothing but dream about. Aw, it wasn't to be; his dreams were filled with those words she left him with, standing there at her door. Usually David slept like a baby nestled in his mother's arms. Not this morning. This morning the dreams that he longed for from night to night were not to be found. He woke in a cold sweat bothered by those words like never before. Those words "Now if you don't mind, get the fuck away from my door and leave me the hell alone" rang in his ears like the bells of Notre-Dame Cathedral in Paris. Those words rang in his ears just as loud and just as strong as those bells.

David rose from his bed, walked to the bathroom, and washed his face in hopes the soap and water would wash the guilt from his face. No matter how hard he scrubbed, he couldn't wash this unfamiliar look from the chiseled manly face. Never before had he experienced this look. David wasn't sure what it was and why he was feeling this way. Why did those simple words hurt so much? How could Tamara have gotten under his skin so much? He who thought women were here for his pleasure and were worth little else. This woman who only knew him as a womanizer, and after today's episode, will never believe he has changed. She could not and would not believe he has fallen in love with her. Throughout his miserable existence, David had thought love was some sort of fable—a myth that did not exist, merely a thought, a fantasy some people made up to give reason to monogamy. David had always felt man was like any other mammal on earth, meant to breed with as many females as possible, much like a dog or cat. So for once in his life, David found himself on unfamiliar ground.

It was ground he knew nothing of. Unsettled was the feeling he faced now. He was lost in emotion that now washed over him like the soapy rag he held in his hand. David washed the soap from the washcloth and rang the water from it and draped it over the shower curtain rod next to his towel. He dried his face and looked down at his watch, expecting it to be well past noon. "Damn it, it's only eleven o'clock. I could have sworn it was later than that. Well shit, Randolph isn't due back until lunchtime. I don't dare show my face downstairs until then. I can't bear to look her in the eyes, knowing what I know now. I can't even attempt to try and explain how I'm feeling. For Christ's sake, I can't explain it to myself. How in the hell can I explain it to her? How can I get her to understand how sorry I am? How can I make her believe I'm not that man who was lurking outside her door? Tamara wouldn't even give me the opportunity to show her I have changed."

How could Tamara dream of such a change in the man she now loved, a man that time and time again has proven himself a pig! Tamara sat on the edge of her bed, wiping the tears from her swollen eyes and letting the tissue clutched in her hand drop after painful drop as she tried holding the tears back. The harder Tamara tried to hold them back, the harder they fell. The tears flowed like small rivers down each cheek of her face. She held the tissues in each hand while wiping first her left cheek then her right. As fast as she pulled another tissue for its box, the faster they were filled with the salty river pouring for her eyes. "Damn him! Damn him to hell. Why did he have to come by the door at that time?" Tamara lifted the tissue to her once again and then looked down at her watch and realized it was time for her to start lunch. She couldn't be late with Mr. Cardigan's lunch again, or he would be very upset with her. "Damn it, he almost made me late for preparing lunch. The last time I was late with Mr. Cardigan's meal, he docked me half a day's pay. I can't afford that. I need to stop blubbering like a baby and get my work done."

She hurried up and washed her face as to not show that she had been crying. As she hung the washcloth on the sink, she heard the car pull up and Justin opening the door. *Shit, he's home early. I hope Mr. Cardigan doesn't expect lunch now. Thanks to David, there is no way now.*

Tamara rushed down to the kitchen and started preparing lunch just in time. She was standing there, peeling potatoes, when Randolph walked through the door. "Mr. Cardigan, I didn't expect you back this soon. Is everything okay?"

"Yes, Tamara, everything is fine and in proper order. Have you seen David lurking around here anywhere?"

"He was in his room the last time saw him. Lunch will be on time, sir. Is there anything else you need?"

"No, I think I am good for now. Well, maybe just one thing. Has David done or said anything to upset you today? I would hate for him to cost me more money."

"No, sir, he has been in his room and I had my work to keep me busy, so we didn't really have time to run into each other. If that's all, I'll finish cooking and serve lunch promptly at noon."

"That's fine, Tamara. I'll see you then."

The door shut, and Tamara finished cooking and readied the cart with the food she had cooked. Tamara rolled the cart out into the dining room as the clock struck twelve o'clock. Randolph and David were seated at the table, patiently waiting. "Aw, thanks, Tamara. What have you prepared for us this afternoon?"

"Well, Mr. Cardigan, with all I had to get done this morning, I didn't really have to time to prepare anything too elaborate. I fixed something simple and filling. Creamed potatoes with garlic and herb butter, chicken fried steak with country gravy and sautéed onions, and for dessert some of that chocolate cake I made last night."

"Very nice. It looks as if we might have to go take a nap after lunch. What do you think, David?"

"Well, I really hope not, Randolph. We have work to get done."

"That's right, we do, don't we, David?"

"Mr. Cardigan, if you don't mind, after lunch I would like Justin to run me into town so I can get a few things."

"Sure thing, Tamara. If you need any money, let me know how much."

"Well, I shouldn't need any, but if I do I will take care of it and give you the receipt when I get back."

"That will be fine, but please make sure to pick up some of that ice cream you got me the last time. David, you will have to try this ice cream. It is the best around. A little shop downtown makes it, and it is simply wonderful."

"I would love to. I love good ice cream."

"*Good* doesn't even come close to describing this ice cream. Tamara always gets me the white chocolate with fudge, and man it is heaven in a bowl. Tamara, get enough for six people. If David likes it as much as I do, we will need it."

"Yes, Mr. Cardigan. I'll make sure to get plenty. I'll clean up and get to town and be back before supper." Tamara left the men to their lunch.

David and Randolph sat there eating in complete silent splendor. The only sounds the two men heard were the sounds of them chewing. Every now and then, Randolph would sigh as he wanted to say something but wasn't quite sure how to word it.

"Randolph, so I take it we will be discussing more murders after lunch as you indicated we would?"

"Well, David, I wouldn't mind taking that nap I spoke about. I know you're eager to finish this and get back to the paper, so yes, we'll start up when we finish."

"Thanks, Randolph. And yes, I would like to get back to the paper and start working on this. Also, I would like to talk to you about something once we settle in for our talk."

"I thought you might. Well, let's finish eating and we'll retire to the library and enjoy a good Havana cigar before we start." David and Randolph finished eating and went over to the library.

"David, would you care for a fine cigar?"

"Yes, I would. I can't remember the last time I had a fine hand-rolled Havana."

"Well, I think I can. It was the day you came to work for me at the paper. During your interview, I offered you one. It kind of stuck in my head because you accepted and asked if it was all right to light up there. That was one of the perks of owning the paper and the building. I didn't have to worry about some smart ass complaining about it. They knew better if they wanted to keep their jobs."

"That's right. I had forgotten all about that day. However nice it is to reminisce about those days, I have something on my mind I wish to ask you about."

"David, I think I know what it is, and I am certain I can't give you the answers to your question just yet. But please ask. I wouldn't want to assume and be wrong, so please ask."

"Randolph, how is it you know so much about me and what I may or may not do? I mean, last night Justin took me home, and he told me not to look for my gun in the nightstand because you had him remove it. If that wasn't enough, he told me what color underwear I had put in my overnight bag. Was it with close circuit cameras and some sort of wireless communication device? I don't buy that psychic shit that Tamara and Justin might believe. I know there has to be something to it."

"Well, David, like I told you, I'm not ready to tell you that yet. Like everything else, you will learn the answers to all your questions prior to leaving Saturday."

"That's something else, Randolph. Why do you think you will die this Saturday? If your illness is in remission, what makes you so certain that you will die this Saturday?"

"Again, David, I am not ready to answer those questions yet. But you can take me at my word when I tell you that I will die at three o'clock this Saturday. That is all I am at liberty to tell you for now, but you will have your answers before I die. That much, David, you can count on."

"I guess I have no choice in this like anything else, do I?"

"No, David, you really do not. So let's get on with our talk.

"Where did I leave off? Oh yeah, I had just told you about the murder of Mrs. Faith Goodwin. Yeah, the first real murder I committed. That one I have a real soft spot for. I guess any serial killer would have a hard-on for their first one. Let me tell you, Faith's death seemed to be the fix I needed. Yes, fix. It was like a drug that I needed and would die if I didn't get it. I can understand why drug addicts are the way they are. At first I thought her murder would be all I would need. For the next three years, I would relive that night over and over again, and at first it was just as intense as it was that night. After a while, the intensity started waning. Then no matter how I replayed the night, it wouldn't bring the feelings back. I found myself thinking about doing it again, so I tried to bury those thoughts again. This time they wouldn't stay hidden in the cemetery of mind. The force behind the emotions hidden within the act was too much to overcome. It wasn't long till I was searching for opportunities and my next victim."

"Randolph, you called yourself a serial killer. Most serial killers fit a pattern, and so do their victims. So far I am not seeing a pattern in the murder or victims. So what makes you a serial killer?"

"Well, David, what would be the perfect serial killer? Wouldn't it be someone whose victims had nothing in common and each act of murder different? Wouldn't that be the true definition of the perfect serial killer?"

"Well, Randolph, that would be the perfect killer, but not a serial killer. A serial killer by definition holds to a predefined pattern. The victims have something in common and hold some meaning to the killer."

"Well, David, maybe I'm not a serial killer. Maybe I am the perfect killer instead. None of my victims had anything in common other than the fact they had to die for my pleasure. They were my drug of choice, as it were. You know what, David. I think I like thinking of myself as the perfect killer. Either case, we need to get on with today's talk or we will not finish this up by Saturday. So please, no more interruptions, if you don't mind.

"Anyway, I started looking for anyone who didn't mean anything to anyone and would not be missed, and I was getting no closer to fulfilling the need growing inside me. I was still selling, but I had left the hardware company and signed on with a pharmaceutical company. Now I was going around to doctor's offices, introducing them to new medications to prescribe to their patients. I studied every medication I was selling. I wanted to know what they did, how they worked. In doing so, I would be able to use them to quench the hunger swelling up inside me. The hunger had to be satisfied one way or another. I found that potassium chloride, if either under prescribed or overdosed, could kill anyone. So I swapped out some of our most commonly used samples with high quantities of potassium chloride. Each of the box's direction was for two tablets four times a day. If I had the potassium chloride milligrams right, then a few people would die within a day or two. As long as I put one sample at each of the doctor's offices, I would decrease the chance of it coming back to me. Who would suspect me in these deaths? All of them would look like natural causes. The people would most likely die in their sleep, and who could ask for more? To die in our beds, painless and unknowing. Now that is the way anyone wants to die.

"I made the change out in five offices over three counties. Again, this would help keep any fingers being pointed at the pharmaceutical rep. My plan was in motion, now to wait. I would hear about the deaths one by one over the radio or in the obituaries. I wasn't sure if this would be the fulfillment my hunger was demanding or if something else would have to be done. It wouldn't be long before I would find out. Within three days, I started hearing about people dying in their sleep from what seemed to be heart failure. The first was an eighty-year-old man. The radio talked about how he was fine the night before and when his daughter went in to wake him for breakfast, she found him dead. The next was a thirty-year-old spinster teacher and how she fell over at her desk during her math class. The third was a forty-four-year-old father of three who was seen clasping his chest while putting shingles on his roof. Number four was a sixteen-year-old cheerleader. While cheering at the big game, she fell from the shoulders of another girl and died on the field. The last was a ninety-eight-year-old great-grandmother who had died at her grandniece's birthday party.

I had killed five people I had never met. This surely would quench the hunger I had been feeling. I couldn't have been more wrong. It seems that when I am wrong, I am really wrong. A month hadn't even passed before those familiar feelings were sneaking back in. This time stronger than ever before. It was as if I had ignored them. I tried to bury them again, but this time it wasn't going to happen. They had found a life of their own because I didn't do as they required in the first place. Now I was a multimurderer and wasn't sure how to feel about that. I started worrying that if I didn't do something to feed the beast growing inside me, it would consume me. I would rather it be fed than to lose myself to it. I found myself looking for someone, someone to become my newest victim. I had to feed the beast. I had no choice in the matter anymore. No one I seemed to run across would do. They were just not what the beast wanted. Until one day, I had been making my normal rounds and ran out of gas between towns. I found myself on the side of the road, waiting for someone to come by and offer help. I knew it could be a while because this road wasn't well traveled. You must be thinking if it isn't used much, then why use it now? Well, it was the shortest route from Kingsport, Tennessee, to Bristol, Tennessee.

I must have waited there for three hours before a car came by. It was a blue '48 Ford pickup. It pulled over, and a massive man rolled down the window and asked if I needed any help. I told him I ran out of gas and had been waiting there for three hours. He offered to siphon some gas out of his tank into mine, and it would get me to the nearest service station. He pulled his truck over close to mine so the tanks would match up and make siphoning from one to the other a bit easier. He was a big man, standing roughly six foot five inches tall, weighing around three hundred and forty pounds if he weighed an ounce. He noticed my black bag in the passenger seat and asked if I was a doctor. I told him I was, and he started telling me about his backache he had for the past week. I told him seeing how he was so kind to stop and help me out, I would give him a shot to help with the pain and for him to rest his back for a few days and he would be fine.

"This was the opportunity I had been searching for. But he was so big. How would I be able to get rid of the body? I damn sure wouldn't be able to lift him, and dragging him was out of the question too. I had learned fire was one of the best ways to cover something up with the killing of Faith Goodwin. But how would I be able to get him somewhere that I would be able to destroy his body or at least make it look like he had died in an accidental fire? I started making small talk to ensure he wouldn't get panicky. I asked him his name. Eugene. Eugene Jefferies, he told me. Mr. Jefferies would be the next priceless work of art I would create. Once Eugene had finished putting gas in my car, I asked him to step to the back of his truck and I would give him the painkiller. He leaned over the tailgate of his pickup, pulled his paints down, and I administered the shot. He stood up and started to walk forward, then he started to weave and stagger. I led him back to his truck and got him to lie down in the bed by telling him he was having a reaction to the medication.

"It wasn't long until Mr. Eugene Jefferies was out cold. I left my car sitting there on the side of the road with the knowledge that no one would be by anytime soon. I drove his truck about half a mile down the road and turned off on to an old dirt road. This road led to an old barn that had been abandoned years ago. I pulled Eugene's truck into the barn then walked back to my car and drove it back up to there. The high weeds and trees hid the barn and my car from the main road, so I could take my time and enjoy the killing of big Eugene. I had the hardest time getting him out of that damn truck, but get him out I did. I stripped his clothes off down to underwear. He was a massive man with a bald head. He looked as if he could have been a linebacker on his high school football team. However, the years had seen his stomach grow rounder and hung over his belt. I had tied his legs together and his arms behind one of the vertical beams still holding up what was left of the roof.

"After about four hours, Eugene started waking up. By now it had started getting dark. There was still a faint bit of light coming into the barn through the holes in the roof. I wasn't worried about light. I had Eugene's truck, and the headlights would shine more than enough light for my needs. Eugene demanded to know why I had him tied up. I said nothing to him for the first few minutes. Then I told him I was going to kill him, and I waited until he was awake so he would know I would be the instrument of his death. At first, he laughed in disbelief, then he struggled against the ropes that bound him. When he could see struggling would do no good, he started pleading for his life. I asked him to shut up and take it like a man. No one should see a man of this size cry, but cry he did.

"I had pictured him a strong man and wasn't expecting him to be a baby about things. Eugene finally stopped crying long enough to ask me why, why him. There was only one response. However, it wouldn't satisfy him if I told him. So I stood there looking at him for a good ten minutes. 'Look, Eugene, it isn't anything you did or didn't do. You were just in the wrong place at the wrong time.' Even that was not enough for him. He started crying again, telling me how he had a wife and five kids. Two boys ages seven and thirteen. Three girls whose ages ranged from two to sixteen. I reckon he thought if he told me how much his family needed him, I wouldn't take his life. A single fact he overlooked was the fact that it had nothing to do with him or his family.

"For a short time, the ugly face of guilt started peeking through the dark recesses of my mind. At one point I was seriously considering letting him go, but as soon as it creeped in, it was gone. I walked around behind Eugene and laid my hand on the top of his head. As I did this, he began shaking and quivering. This brought a whole new feeling up within me. This feeling was much different from the one I had with Faith, and even more so than that of the boy. It wasn't like the adrenalin rush I got when the hammer entered Faith's skull and her blood came oozing up from the hole it created and down her face and into her eyes. It wasn't like the terror I felt when the boy's head popped off and rolled across the hood of my car and I stopped to find his headless corpse lying there by my passenger door.

"It wasn't like anything I had ever felt. I am not sure if I can even explain it well enough to do it justice. Imagine feeling an emotion so powerful the sheer thought of it would drive you to an orgasm. That was how strong this feeling was. I wanted to hold on to it for as long as I could. I walked around to face Eugene and took him by the hair. Lifting his head up so his eyes could meet mine, I told him to keep crying. The sounds of his cries and screams were filling me with this new emotion. Just think of something that could make you feel like a god. That's it. I was feeling like a god, standing there with his life in my hands. I, alone, had the power to take his life or to give it back to him. We know now that there was no chance of giving his life back to him. I wanted to make him think there might have been some kind of chance of me letting him go. I asked him if he could tell me something he had done in his life that meant something.

"Some good deed or life-changing thing he had done that would make him worth saving. He first told me the best thing he had ever done in his pathetic life was fathering his children. 'That's nowhere close enough to save you.' I told him he would need to come up with something better than that if he wanted to live. He then talked about his football days back in high school. Again I told him that would not save him. If he wanted to live, he would have to come up with something powerful to sway me from killing him. He started crying again, saying he had done nothing meaningful enough to save his life. I walked around behind again and told him everyone has done something in their life meaningful enough to warrant living. Some had saved lives, and some changed someone's life for the better. Things like this would save his life, and only things like this would save him.

"He rambled for a few minutes then said he had helped a young man turn his life around. He explained how the young man was heading down a road to prison. If it had not been for Eugene taking him under his wing, the young man would...gasp. Eugene didn't have time to finish his story. I had reached around the post he was tied to. My pocketknife entered his throat on the left side, and I dragged it to the right. While my knife was making its way along the path, my arm was pulling it. It cut through his carotid artery and between the bones of his neck. His blood spilled into his throat, making a gurgling sound as the air from his lungs pushed outward and bubbled up through his blood. I moved back around in front of Eugene to watch the light in his eyes go dim. The pupils dilated and become fixed, just like I had read in the medical books. His blood drained down his neck over his brown overalls, soaking his shirt. The blood turned his overalls a dingy shade of red when the colors mixed.

"Eugene's body sat there, limp, with his head leaned forward and hanging down. His eyes were still open but were no longer seeing anything. Those eyes would never see his children's faces or his wife's tender glances. Never again could those eyes behold the beauty of the world around him. At that moment, I knew the full impact of the new feeling I had. I was a god. For a brief moment, I was a god. I sat there for a good hour, looking at my handiwork. By this time, the darkness of night had fully engulfed the barn, and the brightness of Eugene's headlights filled the barn like the midday sun shining through the windows of house. With Eugene still limp and motionless, I knew I wouldn't be able to get rid of his body like Faith or the young boy. I had to come up with something else—something that would completely hide his body. Aw, shit, I forgot where we were, and sitting there with all the loose straw, it would be too easy to set the barn ablaze.

"I gathered up as much straw and hay as I could fit in my arms and piled it on and around Eugene. I pulled his truck up closer to him so when the flames reached the gas tank, it would explode. I struck a match, bent down, and held it to the dry straw. I figured the dry hay and straw would go up quickly, and I was right. It wasn't long before Eugene's body was fully consumed by fire in a matter of seconds. I ran out of the barn to my car and drove off. I wanted to be as far from the barn as possible before the truck blew up. I was about ten miles down the road when I noticed I had Eugene's blood all over my hands. I pulled off to the side, got out of my car, and walked around to the trunk. I opened it and found the old rags I had there from the last time I fixed a flat tire on my car. I tried to wipe the blood off my hands, but it was already drying. The red juice of Eugene's life was sticky and clumping up on the back of my hands. I got the coffee I was drinking from the cup holder in the front seat and poured it over my hands. The cold coffee was what I needed to loosen the dried blood up enough to enable me to wipe it.

"Well, David, we have reached the end of this one, and it is almost time for dinner. I know you don't want to be late for Tamara's fine food. I bet she has planned something even better for dinner than she fixed for lunch. Once we finish eating, I'll go take a short nap and we'll start up again with another murder around eight o'clock, if that won't be too late for you. The next one might not take that long to tell you about. But be prepared to be up until midnight, and maybe just a bit longer."

"Eight will be fine, Randolph. I am looking forward to hearing more. While you're taking a nap, I'll make some more notes. That way, when I return to the office, I will have all I need to do your stories justice."

"Stories? Is that all you think this is? Some old fucker rambling on about some fairytale stories. I assure you each and every murder happened just as I described to you. Nothing is made up or fabricated. There is a computer in the locked room to the left entrance to the kitchen. I will have Justin meet you there after dinner. Go there and do some investigation of your own. See if I'm lying. See if each of these murders happened or not. Each one will be reported as accidents, and I have told you how each ended so you should be able to match things up."

"Randolph, I didn't mean to imply that you made this shit up, but you have to admit it seems a bit hard to swallow."

"That may be the case, David. However, you need to do this and satisfy yourself that each and every one of these happened the way I say. So meet Justin at the door after we finish dinner. He will let you in and be right there watching your every move. If you so much as try sending a message to someone or signal anyone, Justin will put an end to it as fast as you start it."

"Okay, okay, Randolph. I'll meet Justin and investigate what you have told me so far. I want you to promise me that if I find this to be complete crap, you'll have Justin or Tamara drive me home, and it will be the end of this."

"I can make that promise easily. I know beyond a doubt you'll find everything you need to make you want to stay and hear me out the rest of the way. You won't be able to pass this chance up. But if you don't find what I've told you to be true, I'll send you home with enough money to set you up in New York. An apartment, parking garage, utility bills, and food for two years or until you obtain a new writing job. Whichever comes first, David.

Will that be fair enough payment for the time you have spent here so far?"

"That will be fine, Randolph. It's more than generous compensation for my time."

"Good. This way, you won't feel like I am just some old fucker holding you hostage to force you to listen to me ramble. You need to realize that if Justin thinks you're trying to contact someone to help you leave here without my permission, he will end your time online real fast."

"What good would it do me to attempt to contact anyone for help? I don't have a damn clue where the hell I am anyway."

"Well, you might think someone can trace your whereabouts. I can promise you that won't possible. When I had the phone system installed, I made sure that it was set up to where it would be nearly impossible to track it back to this location."

"You do realize a statement like that one makes men in my field curious to the point we investigate till we find out why."

"Yes, I know that, and you won't be able to find anything out of the ordinary. I suggest you spend your time checking out the things we've discussed and verifying the information I have provided you with to date. I'm tired and a bit frustrated with you at this moment, so I will go take my nap and see you at dinner. Justin has my instruction and is waiting for you. This is your one and only chance to get online, so I recommend you make the best of the time you have."

David sat there for a second as Randolph left the library for his bedroom. "Damn old goat. Is he trying to entice me into trying to contact someone or what? I doubt if he has gone to the extremes he described, security like that would cost him a bundle. The question is, why would he tell me this, knowing who I am and my inquisitive nature?" David finished his cigar and was about to go meet Justin when Justin came into the room.

"Are you ready to head over to the computer room, Mr. Erwin?"

"Yes, Justin, I am ready. I was just finishing my smoke. If there is something else you need to do, I can wait for a short bit."

"No, sir. I was told by Mr. Cardigan that you need to do this now and not to allow you to put it off. So if you are ready, we can go."

David and Justin walked out to the main entry room and over to a door David had not noticed before. It was smaller than the other doors in the house. Even though it was painted like wood, it was a metal door. David wasn't sure how he had overlooked this door. It stood out like a naked man at a wedding. The door handle was a simple and normal round handle, much like the ones on the doors in David's house. As David was studying the door, Justin reached into his breast pocket and retrieved a solitary key and unlocked the door.

Justin opened the metal door and reached inside to find the light switch. When the lights came on, David caught a faint smell of old cigar smoke. The stale old smoke hung in the air much like mist forms an early morning fogs. "Justin, does Randolph come in here often?"

"Mr. Erwin, I can't say if he does or he doesn't because I don't know. I am only here when he needs me to drive him somewhere. Other than that, I do as I please until Mr. Cardigan needs me. Please go in and do what you need to do. I would like to leave soon. It's nearing my time to go."

David walked in and found a small old gray metal desk with an old desktop computer sitting on it. "Damn, you would think with Randolph's money and the amount he had to have spent on this room, he would have at least bought a decently new computer."

"Mr. Erwin, please."

"Yes, Justin, I'm going." The walls of the room were covered in gray paint, leaving David with the feeling as if he was in a metal room. David scratched his head, wondering why Randolph went to these extremes for this one room. It just didn't fit with how the rest of the house was decorated in the medieval motif. David thought how strange this was. A room that didn't match any part of the house. Maybe Randolph meant what he said about no one being able to track anything back to the house.

David sat down at the metal desk and booted up the computer. David was surprised to find the machine was faster than he had anticipated. In a matter of seconds, David was online and searching the web for evidence to support or disprove Randolph's claims. David logged into the missing persons website and searched for people missing around 1964 when Randolph said he had hit the retarded boy. The computer started clicking away, and suddenly the web paged loaded, and there was a report of a missing retarded fourteen-year-old boy. The report stated the boy was prone to walking off from his mother's house but usually would be found picking flowers near the road at Mr. Wilson's farm. Investigators found blood on the ground and the fence post but weren't sure if it was from the boy or from local wildlife. "Damn, if the rest match like this one does, I might just have the making of a bestselling book based on Randolph's lengthy murderous life."

David moved his attentions toward Mrs. Faith Goodwin's death. Back to the missing persons site, and David typed in Faith's name and waited the few seconds for the page to load. There was a picture matching the description Randolph depicted in his tales of her death. The report read, "Mrs. Faith Goodwin was found burned to death when her car went through the guardrail and plummeted some one hundred feet down to the rocky base below."

"Well shit, two for two. It seems Randolph's stories are true.

However, are they his tales from his life or just things he read about and is now recounting them as his own? Only time will tell."

"Mr. Erwin, are you almost done? I really need to be going."

"Yes, Justin, I'm almost done. I have just two more things to look up and we can go." David searched for the deaths of those persons Randolph said he had swapped out medicines and they died from what seemed to be heart attacks. As David waited for the next page to load, his mouth was watering with the thoughts of money a book based on these deaths could bring, and even more importantly, the fame. A link to a newspaper article about the deaths of some five men, women, and children that seemed to have died from heart attacks. The writer indicated he thought these deaths might have been connected. The article described each death was in a different town and had different doctors. Even with these facts present, the writer still felt the deaths were connected somehow. He just couldn't figure out what the connection could be.

"Three for three. This is starting to show promise. If this last one comes out as depicted by Randolph, then we have the makings of a great book." David typed out the name Eugene Jefferies in the search box, along with the year 1968. The screen displayed the results in the usual speed, and David was pouring over each link's description when he found a link to what appeared to be a police report. He clicked on the link and was taken to an old report from Wash Woods, Virginia. The report from the constable stated Samuel Murphy's old barn had been set on fire by what appeared to be Eugene Jefferies. He had fallen asleep with a lit cigarette. Both the old barn and Eugene were lost. Samuel had agreed not to ask Eugene's family to pay for the barn and the damage Eugene caused. David was not surprised with the report. He would have been more shocked if he had not found this. It all seemed to fit too good.

"Are you finished yet, Mr. Erwin? Mr. Cardigan will be expecting you soon."

"Yes, Justin, I am done. We can go now." Justin waited by the door as David walked out and over to the dining room to meet Randolph for dinner. David arrived just as Tamara wheeled the dinner cart in from the kitchen. "Sorry it took me so long, Randolph. There was tons of information on the subjects you and I have been discussing. I wanted to make sure everything matched up."

"That's okay, David. I expected it might take you a little while to confirm everything. I hope all doubt has been removed from your mind and we can continue without any further interruptions."

"Randolph, I am sure those are gone for good. It seems you have been telling me the truth; and with that, I am willing to write this for you and tell your story in the manner deserving of your life."

"Thanks, David. Now let's eat this fine dinner Tamara has prepared for us. It would be rather rude if we continued to talk shop and didn't enjoy Tamara's hard work."

"I agree, Randolph, Tamara's hard work needs to be the center of attention and not work. Speaking of which, could she join us for once?"

"David, that is a very good idea. She should grace us with her presence and enjoy her hard work, as we do. Tamara, I insist you join us, so please set another place."

"Mr. Cardigan, since joining your employment, you have never asked me to join you."

"This mistake I am now correcting. So please, if you don't mind, join us. I am sure David would enjoy your company over mine any day."

"To tell you the truth, Randolph, I would much rather her

company over yours or anyone else's. Tamara is a welcome sight for these old eyes. Tamara, please join us for dinner."

"Okay, I will get another place setting and I'll join you."

David, Randolph, and Tamara sat there enjoying their meal, and for the first time in a long time, Randolph was laughing. Randolph leaned back in his chair and thought back, searching his brain for the last time he had enjoyed people this much. The only thoughts of enjoyment seemed to always come from the death of others. He couldn't recall any time in his entire life where he sat around with others and just laughed. He couldn't even remember moments even close to this, not even from his childhood. Tamara noticed a tear streaming down from Randolph's right eye.

"Mr. Cardigan, is everything all right?"

"Yes, Tamara, everything is fine. I just can't remember when I have laughed this much or had this much fun, and it makes me happy to laugh with you and David."

"I know since I've been here, Randolph, you haven't laughed at all, or at least that I could hear."

"David, I don't usually have much of a reason to laugh."

The three finished eating and joking around. David was telling stories from his hay days as a criminal writer in New York. Tamara told stories of her days in the business world. She recounted a day where her boss came into her office and threatened to fire her if she didn't have a report on his desk before five o'clock and how she slapped him across the cheek and walked out. Before she reached the elevator, he was on his knees, begging her to come back. He even gave her twice her pay if she would stay. Tamara went on to tell about them how she told him to fuck off and left. That day, she went to Walmart and got a job as a cashier. As for Randolph, he just sat there, listening and smiling. He never once offered up a story from his past. Each time Tamara would ask, he would only say "that's too boring, no one would enjoy it" and would leave it at that.

Once the three were done with their meals, Tamara cleared the table and excused herself. David and Randolph sat there for a few minutes when Randolph recommended they retire to the library for their evening meeting.

"Randolph, can we get in more than one murder tonight? I think it might be best seeing how we will end..."

"Shush. Tamara might hear, and I do not want her to know any of this. Is that clear?"

"Yes, sir, it is perfectly clear."

The two men went to the library and took their seats. David then again started to ask Randolph if they would be able to discuss more than one killing from now on so they would be able to finish up everything Randolph wanted to complete within the next few days.

"A lot will depend on how I feel. I can't promise, but I will try. But I will do what I can, David."

"I can't ask for more than that."

"Where did I leave off? Oh yeah, I know. I had just finished telling you about the death of Eugene Jefferies. By the way, David, did you check into those deaths?"

"Yes, Randolph. I was able to verify all the information you gave me. I must say, I had my doubts. I fully expected to find some fake websites made to look authentic. I found newspaper reports, police reports, and missing person's files. I have no choice to accept each and every one is real."

"Good. We will have no more of this nonsense and doubting my word. I know in your line of work it is natural to disbelieve everything until proof can be obtained.

"Well, David, it would be another two years before the itch would start to hit me again. It seemed like as long as I ran a hands-on approach to killing, I wouldn't so much as think of death or killing for two years. It was now the summer of 1966, and the job selling pharmaceuticals wasn't for me. I just couldn't see myself pushing drugs for the rest of my life. I gave my notice and started looking for a new job. I applied to every hardware manufacturer in the country and nothing. I was out of work for about a month and damn near ready to get a job bagging groceries at the newly opened Piggly Wiggly. Things were getting pretty rough for me with no income flowing in. I finally got a call from a trucking company. They wanted me to do outside sales for them. I didn't recall sending them my résumé or applying with them in any form. I decided to call them back and see where it might go.

"They offered me a position selling their services in the tri-state area. I would have to drive a truck from time to time in order to show clients what type of equipment we had and the quality and service we stood for. The very first week with them, I was in training. I was training to drive a big rig. They figured I would be able to sell their services better if I knew how to drive and what the equipment would be capable of. After training, I was sent out with a trucker for a week so I would understand the exact nature of the service they provided.

"I tell you, that was an adventure. I went all over the country. We hauled loads from Trenton, Pennsylvania, to San Diego, California. We hit every mountain pass along the Rockies from Donner's Pass, Elk Mountain, and Cabbage Patch. We didn't miss a beat. I was actually starting to think maybe I wanted to drive for a living. Then the itch started coming back. I was starting to feel those familiar cravings—the ravenous hunger for death, my bloodthirsty lust for watching the life leave someone's eyes as they slipped into the eternal darkness of death. Whether they left this world and entered heaven or hell wasn't my concern. That was between them and their maker. I was just providing the method by which they would meet. By this time, I was all too used to these feelings and almost had them timed. I would have liked it to have hit me when I was closer to the area I knew. But things like this can't be controlled, much less held back.

"I was sure at some point I would give into those feelings, but when? How would I break away if I needed to satisfy my lusty hunger? Like old grim reaper himself, I had no choice but to give in. My trainer and I were on the back roads of Indiana near Gary when the feelings reached the apex. We were stopped for the night near a honkytonk, and he had gone in for a few drinks. After a couple of hours, I saw him come out and get into a car with a young lady. That old scoundrel had found a piece of ass to spend the night with. I sat there for a few more hours watching people enter and leave the place. Finally, a young man walked out and started walking down the road. I waited for a few minutes before I started the truck and slipped it into gear. I let it roll slowly down the road, and I could see he had turned down a dirt road heading east. I followed for a mile or more to make sure no one from the honkytonk could see what I was about to do. Once I was certain no one else was around or would be able to tell what was about to occur, I proceeded with my plan.

"I could see him standing there, smoking a cigarette as if to catch his breath for a few minutes. I put the truck into gear and pushed the fuel pedal to the floor. I was shifting when I saw him bend over, facing the direction I was coming from. I think he was fixing his boots. Just as he bent his head backward to see what was making the noise, the grille of the truck collided with his face, knocking him backward. I looked into my side mirrors for the body and couldn't see anything. I turned the truck around so I could get a better look. The body had to be there somewhere. Just then, I heard what sounded like a scream coming from the front underside of my truck. I stopped and put the truck into reverse, then I set the brakes and climbed out of the cab. Right there, not more than ten feet in front of the bumper, was the body of the drunk young man.

"I quickly grabbed some old white sheets from the storage area under the bunk and went back to the body. I stopped for a second because I thought I heard him groan. I looked around to make sure no one was anywhere close. I laid the sheets down on the ground beside the young man and reached my hand under his head to pick it up. As I lifted it, my hand sank into the soft tissue of his brain. I could feel the jagged edges of bone that used to be his skull. I rolled him over on his side to find the most shocking sight. Everywhere I placed my hand, I couldn't feel any skin. I only felt muscle and bone. I decide to roll him over so I could get a better look at my handiwork. The sight was so disturbing, I had to turn and vomit. There was nothing left, nothing at all. The skin was totally removed from his back. The back of his skull was missing. His backbone was exposed. Where there should have been muscle and skin covering it, there was nothing. It was as if he was a skeleton with small bits of meat and blood hanging off each vertebra.

"I pushed the sheets underneath the body, knowing full well the blood would soak through. I was searching my memory for a spot I could dump the body where it would be a few days, at the very least, until someone would find it. I looked around for anything, any body parts to make sure I left nothing behind. I wrapped him up in the sheets and tied it tight with some hemp rope I found lying near where I found the sheets. At first glance, he almost looked like a Christmas present lying there, all red and white with the green tint of the hemp. Yes, it was a Christmas present, an early one for me. Just then, I heard the sound of water flowing. This could be the perfect place to dump him. The water might wash him downstream, far enough to allow me and my trainer to get down the road a few hundred miles.

"In the morning, my trainer came back and woke me up so we could hit the road. We left out and stopped about four hours south of Indianapolis just before the Kentucky state line to get some lunch. While we were there sitting at the lunch counter, they had the midday news playing on the radio. The reporter was talking about a car accident where some teenagers tried to outrun a train and lost the race. Three were killed, and one was in the hospital in critical condition. Just then, the report switched the topic to a young boy that was fishing and found a body wrapped up in some old sheets. The body looked as if it had been dragged down a rocky dirt road. The police were trying to identify the man, but with the body in the shape it was in, they doubted if identification would be possible.

"I don't know if hearing it on the radio made me feel better about leaving him floating in the river in the blood-soaked sheets or knowing people now knew without knowing I had killed someone. I wasn't sure. All I knew was something had changed with the hunger inside me. It was satisfied in a way it had never been before. Yes, the hunger was fulfilled with the death of the man, but it was still different. I couldn't describe what the difference was. I didn't know how to explain it. It was like the satisfaction a kid gets when he gets that special present he just had to have for Christmas. It wasn't for a few years that I started to understand it.

"Another two years passed, and the hungry feeling didn't return. I thought maybe for a little while that the hunger would never return. Could it be I would never have the need to kill again? Would I be able to lead a normal life, maybe settle down with a pretty girl and have a house full of kids? Normal, what is normal? Who was to say I wasn't normal? Who was to say the hunger wasn't a normal part of my psychological makeup? I found myself missing the hunger. I had grown to expect it, even wanting it. What would I do with this part of my life missing? What if I killed again? Maybe the hunger would return. I started thinking all kinds of thoughts. I finally realized that killing wouldn't bring the hunger back. Killing was what satisfied the hunger. Killing was what the hunger needed to settle it down. Well, if killing wouldn't bring the hunger back, what would if anything?

"I came to the conclusion the hunger would have to come back on its own or not come back. So I would keep working and living my mundane existence. If the hunger returned, it returned. If not, then not. Either case, I couldn't force it or wait on it. Life must go on. I decided to put it out of my mind and concentrate on my job. I had left the trucking company and found me a job selling newspaper ad spaces. I was traveling all over the tri-state area. This was how I broke into the newspaper industry and started building my wealth and business. I saved every penny I could and worked my ass off to sell ad space. Before long, I was able to get a bank loan to buy my first paper. It took me another three years of hard work to build the paper up to be the largest and most respected in the area. Even though I didn't know anything about writing or what good news was, I built it up from almost nothing to a multimillion-dollar company in a very short time.

"Five years had passed and still the hunger had not returned. I thought I might have replaced it with a new hunger—a hunger for money. The Vietnam War was going strong, and hippies were protesting in the streets. Everything that makes paper sell. I had gone from damn near a pauper to a millionaire and was respected throughout the industry as a powerhouse. I had bought up several papers on the verge of collapse and built them all into a network worth close to thirty million dollars. I was living the life, going where I wanted, when I wanted. Everything was going great, and I didn't need any interruption that could cause my plans to go off-kilter.

"Things were going so well I decided to settle down and have a family. I had met a fine woman, and we had been dating for several months. Martha Ruth Needles was her name. She was about as pretty as a newborn puppy and innocent to boot. I took Martha to her favorite restaurant and had the chef place the engagement ring I had bought on top of the black cherry cheesecake she always ordered for dessert. We ate dinner pretty much like we always had, and when it came time for dessert, Martha told the waiter she didn't want any. I was flabbergasted. She had always ordered the same things each and every time, and if she didn't this time, how would I pop my surprise on her? I asked her why she wasn't getting her favorite dessert and she said, 'I need to watch my girlish figure.' I stated that she need not watch her figure because I was doing that for her. She blushed and stated she had gained some weight.

"I said, 'Balderdash' and then told the waiter to bring two slices of that delectable black cherry cheesecake and nodded to the maître d'. Martha insisted that she didn't need all that fattening food. I told her to hush the talk about getting fat. She was beautiful, sexy, and all any man could ever want. The waiter brought the cheesecake and set mine down, then Martha's. We picked up our forks at the same time and I took a bite. Martha let her fork slide through the tip end of the delicious dessert and looked down. As she saw the ring sitting atop the cheesecake, resting on a cherry, she almost fainted. I reached for her arm and she said, 'Randolph, yes, yes, yes.'

"We were married in the spring and had planned our honeymoon for Paris, France. We had planned to take a luxury liner over to Paris. While we were boarding the ship, some old lady came over and offered roses for me to purchase for my beautiful wife. As my hand touched the old woman's, she grabbed my hand and stared me right in the eyes. Her face went from a joyous smile to that of sheer terror. The fear washed over her face like rain on a windowpane. Not even the nightmares of Charles Manson could compare to the fear in her eyes. She handed me a red rose with yellow tips. 'This one will suit your lovely wife, sir. Please accept it for your wife with my compliments.' As I took the rose, the old woman turned to Martha and whispered something to her.

"Later that evening, as Martha and I were getting dressed for dinner, I asked her what the old woman whispered to her. Martha looked at me then said, 'She told me I would die before reaching my destination and you would be my killer. Isn't that something to tell someone on their honeymoon? I wanted to tell her that I was married to the most wonderful, sweetest, kindhearted man in the world. But I decided to pretend to hear her and forget about it.' We finished dressing and went to the main dining room where we were to be seated at the captain's table. While we sat there eating, I couldn't help but to think of what the old woman told Martha. Why would she say that to Martha? What did she know that I didn't know? Would the hunger come back and take Martha from me? Could I really kill my beautiful wife?

"Later that night, Martha and I were walking along the main deck, enjoying the moonlight bouncing off the darkened water of the Atlantic Ocean. Martha got up on the rail and leaned forward ever so slightly. Her hands grasped the rail as if her life depended on it. I asked Martha to step down away from the rail because I thought it was unsafe. In the back of my head, I had pictured pushing on her back strong enough to cause her to tilt over the rail and fall into the midnight-black waters below. From the height above the water where we were standing, no one would have heard the screams and the sudden splash caused by her body colliding with the dark waters beneath the ship.

"I shook my head and excused myself and walked inside to the men's restroom. I went to the sinks and washed my face and hands. Even though the thought had entered my mind, the hunger to go through with it wasn't there. For this reason, I knew I would not kill my sweet Martha. The hunger had always been the driving force behind me killing. It would get so strong I couldn't hold it back and had to satisfy it. There was no driving force this time, no overwhelming urge to take someone's life. I knew without this behind me forcing me to kill, I would never kill my beloved Martha. Feeling better that the thoughts weren't part of the hunger emerging, I walked back to the deck where I left Martha. As I got closer to the spot where I had left her standing only moments ago, I could see people gathering. I pushed my way through to find my Martha lying on the deck in a pool of blood. I screamed and dropped to my knees beside her lifeless body.

"I knelt there beside her, holding her hand, crying out, 'No.' She had been struck in the head by a golf ball. It would seem the captain liked to practice his swing at night when there were fewer passengers roaming the decks. Unfortunately for Martha, his swing went a bit wild that night and his ball had struck her in the right temple, killing her instantly. The only solace I could find was that she didn't feel any pain and died quickly. The captain had the ship pulled into port that very night. The police came aboard and took statements from everyone who was there, including me. The captain was taken into custody and questioned then released the next morning. Once the ship returned to our departure point, the company relieved the captain of his duties. I was given a written apology by the company and offered to pay for Martha's funeral. I found that to be an insult and had my attorneys file suit. Once everything was done, it went to court and the jury awarded me one and half million dollars for wrongful death.

"Again I found myself alone and working till all hours of the night. One night, I decided to take a drive in the country to clear my head and try to get the memories of Martha's death out of my head. I had been driving for around three or four hours, and the sun was starting to break over the horizon when I saw someone standing on the side of the road hitchhiking. I stopped and asked him where he was going. He replied north. North was just the direction I was heading in. It wouldn't be long till the hunger started creeping up from the darkest recesses of my mind. I started glancing over at my passenger and thinking how I could cause his death. With each slanting glance, the man seemed to squirm in the seat. He finally asked me where I was heading. I guess this was an attempt to make small talk and help him feel me out. I told him I was just out driving to clear my head. I had had a rough day and needed to get away from the office, and I wasn't heading toward anywhere in particular.

"We sat there riding for a bit, and I asked him where he was heading. Again he muttered north. I stated that north was a very big place and I needed to know where to drop him off in the north. Was it the North Pole, North Hampton, northern Virginia, where would he like to go?

'Just north. Anywhere north will do. Just drop me wherever and whenever.'

"The longer we drove, the more I thought of ways to kill this odd man going to north nowhere. Stabbing him crossed my mind, but I didn't have a knife. Running him down with my car started to seem like the most likely way. However, this would not give me the hands-on experience that I was thirsting for. Nothing I came up with would do. Too many options might leave evidence or even a witness, and I could not have this. I drove for another few miles when we came across a small out-of-the-way diner. I pulled off and told the guy I was going to get a bite to eat and he was welcome to join me if he wished. He shook his head no and said he would just get out here and be on his way. He thanked me for the ride and walked off. I went into the diner and sat down. A young pretty brunette with a slender build and a nice rack walked over to take my order. I sat there for a few seconds, looking at her tits and how they protruded out from her low-cut top.

"I ordered coffee and she walked off. I sat there studying the menu as if I was lost inside the pages of a great book. The waitress showed up a few minutes later with my coffee and asked if I was ready to order. I told her what I wanted wasn't on the menu, but I would try and find something to replace it with. However, I doubted if I would be able to find anything as sweet and delicious as she was. She smiled and told me she wasn't on the menu; but if I played my cards right, she might have another menu for me to look at later where she could be found on it. I said I couldn't wait to view the other menu, but for now I would have a slice of apple pie and one scoop of chocolate ice cream. As she walked back to fill my order, her ass was swinging side to side and reminded me of a swing on some child's playground, swinging up high on one side and low on the other then switching like some pendulum on a grandfather clock. When she returned, she placed the plate containing my order in front of me, along with a napkin with the word *menu* written on it. I took my fork and scooped into the pie and ice cream for my first bite. Then I picked up the napkin and unfolded it to see the words 'Off in an hour, then the real dessert can be yours.' She also wrote that she wanted me to meet her out back and we could go somewhere.

"I finished my pie and walked up to the counter to pay the older lady standing there. I gave her the ticket and asked where my waitress went so I could leave her a tip. The old lady told me she had left for the day, and I could leave the tip with her and she would make sure Sally got it. I gave her the price of the pie and ice cream and left her with a two-dollar tip for Sally and left. I got in my car and drove around to the side where Sally was waiting there, smoking a cigarette. She opened the passenger side door and climbed inside. I asked her where to, and she replied, 'Head south about three miles then turn left on to the side road. Then there would be a motel off to the right.' We pulled out of the parking lot of the diner and headed south. In about three miles, I turned on to the side road she told me about. The entire time we drove, we said nothing to each other. I thought this was quite weird that two people heading to an out-of-the-way cheap ass roach motel to have sex spoke not even one word. I pulled into the parking lot of the motel, and Sally told me to go around back and pull in front of the last door. I asked her what was going on and how did I know I wasn't about to be robbed or worse, considering we had not spoken two words between us. Sally said, 'Mister, I don't want your money or anything else. I only want a good fuck, and if you're not ready to provide me with that then leave.'

'No, no. I'm ready to give you that and much, much more.'

'Then do as I told you.' I drove around the building and parked in front of the last door. 'Wait here and I'll get the key. By the way, the room will cost twenty-five dollars, and I hope you're not expecting me to pay for it.' I handed her two bills a twenty and a five to cover the cost of the room. I sat there for a few minutes while Sally went to pay for the room and get the key. While waiting, the haunting hungry feeling hit me like a brick to the back of my head. I wasn't sure if I would be able to hold back until we got in behind the closed door of the motel room. Sally came walking down the sidewalk, sporting a huge smile on her face. It reminded me of the old saying 'smiling like the cat that ate the canary.' She walked up and unlocked the door and motioned for me to join her inside.

"Once we were behind the closed door, Sally stripped off her clothes to reveal those tits that were protruding out of her low-cut top. They stuck out and held their shape as if they were plastic. There she stood, buck ass naked as my eyes worked their way along her body and outlining every curve. She was almost perfect. No hair shown anywhere other than her pubic area. I felt the swelling building inside my pants as she walked over to me. 'I see you're not dead from the waist down.' She let her hand rub the front of my pants.

'No, ma'am, I'm far from dead in that area.' Suddenly, she undid my belt and lowered my zipper. My pants fell to the floor as she worked the buttons on my shirt to remove it and dropped it on the floor by my feet. I stepped out of my pants and started to lean in and kiss her. She pulled back and shook her finger from side to side. 'No, no. Kissing is for those I love, and you are just a fuck. The only place you can kiss me is between my legs and maybe my tits.'

"I thought this was a bit odd, as well; but so far there wasn't anything about Sally that seemed normal. She took my hand and led me over to the bed and laid me down. She then started kissing me in areas that I had not been kissed in years. As she was kissing me, my mind wandered back to Mrs. Goodwin and her delicious end with that hammer. I found myself wishing for that hammer now. To have a double explosion of the highest pleasures in my life. Aw, this was not to be. There wasn't a hammer or anything else I could use. She stopped kissing me just short of me climaxing and said, 'No, no you ain't getting off that way, or at least not until I get mine. Too many times I've gotten you men off, and each time I was left wanting and having to take care of my own needs. So you'll have to earn yours by making sure I get mine and then some before you can get yours.'

"With her saying that, I grabbed her and threw her to the bed and took her clothes and tied her legs to the end of the bed. 'Kinky. I like kinky.' I tied her wrists to the bed, and I started kissing her breasts and stomach. I then moved down to the fur-covered area she was dying for me to kiss. As my tongue did its magical work, she squirmed and bucked with each and every touch. When she finally reached her climax, she screamed out, 'Oh God, oh shit, oh fuck.' I climbed on top of her, and as I started to penetrate her, I reached for her panties and slid them under her neck. 'What are you doing?' she asked between her moans.

'I am going to strangle you, cutting off the oxygen to your brain and causing your death just in time for my climax.' She started bucking harder, trying to throw me off her, hoping to keep me from killing her. But the more she fought, the more excited I became. As I tightened her panties around her neck and started pulling them tighter, her eyes bulged outward more and more. Just as my body exploded inside of hers, the light inside her eyes dwindled until there was no more light.

"I rose from the bed and left her laying there tied up. I carefully removed anything that might indicate I was there. As far as the hotel was concerned, she was alone. This was all the registration book would show and all the police would see. So there would be little, if anything, that could point out anyone, much less me. I put my clothes on and tidied the room up a bit. I wiped down all the surfaces to make sure my fingerprints wouldn't be found. Then I opened the door with my shirt and closed it behind me. I got into my car and drove off. I drove back home with the hunger filled. I was glad I didn't have a hammer this time. It seemed more personal, less bloody, but just as fulfilling as the first one I strangled.

"Well, Mr. Erwin, it would seem I have been a bit long-winded tonight and talked right through my bedtime."

"Randolph, you said it was just as fulfilling as the first one you strangled. Who and when did you first strangle?"

"Good night, Mr. Erwin." Randolph left the room and left David wondering about the first one.

"Damn it, he just loves to leave me hanging like this. No matter. Tomorrow I will nail him down for the answers I want."

David sat back in the high-back leather chair, puffing on the last remnants of his hand-rolled Cuban cigar. The smoke circled upward toward the yellow-stained ceiling. David thought for a second that it must have taken years of smoking for the ceiling to have become that stained from the smoke. "I am just going to have to tie Randolph down to get the answers I'm looking for." David rose from his chair and started to walk toward the door leading to the entry hall when he heard a noise coming from the kitchen. "She can't be working this late." David walked over to the door where the sounds were coming from. As he reached out to push the door open, it suddenly swung inward. A deep startling half scream, half gasp pierced David's ears as Tamara appeared in the doorway.

"Mr. Erwin, you startled me. I thought you and Mr. Cardigan had gone to bed and I could finish cleaning up."

"Well, Randolph went upstairs a few minutes ago, and I was just sitting here finishing my cigar before retiring for the night. I heard a noise coming from the kitchen and walked over to see what it was. I was certain that you had gone to bed by now and thought maybe Randolph might have sneaked back around for a snack or something and I could corner him for answers to some of my questions."

"No, it was just me, Mr. Erwin. Mr. Cardigan never comes back down after heading off to bed. He eats his three square meals and maybe a dessert at dinnertime, but never a midnight snack."

"Yeah, I am like that as well. I eat the normal meals and sometimes a dessert if I find something that hits my fancy, but never anything after dinner."

"You and Mr. Cardigan seem to have more in common than I thought."

"How so, Tamara? What similarities do Randolph and I share?"

"Mr. Erwin, it's not so much similarities that you and Mr. Cardigan share as it is more like the way you two talk and act. Yes, there are some things you and Mr. Cardigan do alike that could make someone think you and he are one person, but we both know this isn't the case. Mr. Cardigan is a good forty years older than you. Maybe someone like me could mistake you for father and son. One time I heard Mr. Cardigan raise his voice to you and you raised yours to him, and the first thing that hit me was that you two fought like father and son. If I didn't know better, I would believe that you were the same person."

"Tamara, what could make you think that? You, yourself, said Randolph has a good forty years on me."

"I know, Mr. Erwin, but when I hear you two talk from behind the kitchen door, it almost seems like one voice."

"Damn it, girl, you're now telling me that I sound like an old man. That isn't even right."

"No, Mr. Erwin, I am not saying that at all. However, you and Mr. Cardigan's voices do sound a lot alike, and sometimes I have to open the door to see which one of you two is talking."

"Now, now, you know Randolph and I don't sound anything alike. I can't see how you or anyone else could get us confused. Well, it doesn't really matter, I guess, but there is a question I have for you."

"Yeah, Mr. Erwin, and what would that be?"

"Since I've been here, you have always referred to Randolph and me as Mr. Cardigan and Mr. Erwin. Is this out of some misguided respect or something?"

"Not at all, Mr. Erwin. I know you told me to call you David, and every now and then I slip and call you that. Then I remember that Mr. Cardigan instructed me to refer to you and him by your surnames at all times. When I asked him why, he just gave me a hard look and told me to just do it. Seeing how I was pretty much ordered to use the surnames of you both, that is what I must do."

"That makes no sense at all. Why would Randolph ask you to refer to us by our surnames? I just can't understand that."

"Well, Mr. Erwin, it might be so you and he do not get confused when I call you by your first names when both of you are in the room at the same time. I don't really know why he asked me to do that, but he does pay me so I must do as he asks."

"Tamara, how could Randolph and I get confused on which one of us you would be talking to when my first name is David and his is Randolph."

"It's easy, Mr. Erwin. You and Mr. Cardigan both share the same first name. Like you, his first name is David and his middle is Randolph."

"That's odd. David Randolph Cardigan and David Randolph Erwin. Who would have thought our first and middle names were both the same? The only difference is I hate my middle name, and it seems Randolph likes his."

"Just the opposite, Mr. Erwin. Mr. Cardigan hates Randolph. Before you came into the house, he always insisted that I call him David."

"I guess you could be right, Tamara. It makes sense he would have me call him Randolph and not David. It would be somewhat awkward for me to hear myself saying David all the time when I was talking to Randolph."

"You think it would be awkward for you, how about when I would hear it? I wouldn't know who was talking to whom. So, Mr. Erwin, you see how there are similarities between you and Mr. Cardigan."

"Yes, Tamara, I can see where there might be a few things that we have in common, but we are still two very different men. Good night, dear lady. Sleep well and sweet dreams."

With those last words, David walked out of the room and disappeared behind the closed door of his bedroom. How he wished he had spoken to Tamara about how he felt about her and how he longed to hold her and kiss those soft lips. David fell asleep with these thoughts running through his mind. "Tomorrow, yeah, tomorrow I'll tell her everything. Tomorrow I'll pull her aside and make her understand how wrong I was and how stupid I have been. Yeah, tomorrow I'll let sweet Tamara know I love her."

After being left at the door entering the kitchen, Tamara turned and went back to her work. "Could he be the man I've waited for, or is he just one more who wants nothing more than a quick lay and be done with me? Can I afford to find out this time?"

In the shadows, standing out of sight, Randolph overheard Tamara talking to herself. "I know I should let her know everything. I know I should, but I can't. It wouldn't change anything. The end results will still be the same. But how can I not forewarn her of the events that will take place in the few days? Is it fair to her to allow things to continue on its natural path and not at least give the innocent the chance to change their own paths?" Randolph stood there, hiding in the shadows, watching Tamara as she finished her work. His eyes were filled with a sad, tearful look. The look told volumes where words would fall short of describing what was hidden in his mind.

Once Tamara had finished cleaning the kitchen and left for her bedroom, Randolph walked over to the refrigerator and removed the ice cream in the freezer and slowly pulled a spoon from the dishwasher, taking great care to make no noise as the spoon pulled free. He stood there running the spoon across the top of the frozen creamy chocolate goodness and lifting it up to his mouth. With each bite, Randolph's eyes lightened up, and a smile came across his face much like that of a small child. But after each bite, the sad look would return. It was as if the sweet taste of chocolate wiped away the sadness for a brief instance then returned once the sweet flavor was gone. Randolph turned and put the ice cream back into the freezer then washed the spoon, leaving little to no evidence that he was there. He slowly crept back to his room for the night.

The next morning, David awoke like he had for the past few days he had been trapped in this house. The house that looked like a rundown, broken-down plantation house of the old South. As David readied himself for what he knew would be a taste sensation, his mouth watered just as it had done since the first bite he had tasted of Tamara's cooking. As the washcloth wiped across his eyes and washed away the sleep, David heard the faint sounds of what seemed like a car driving off. He went to the window and peered out through the dirty grimy glass but didn't see anything. Nothing, not even the smallest amount of dust that would have been stirred up by the wheels if any had driven away from the house. David shook his head, noting that his ears were playing tricks on him. Walking back over to the bed where his clothes were laid out waiting on him, he thought he heard the soft sounds of a car again. "Not this time. I'm not falling for it again. If there is a car driving off, then it can just keep going. Today is the tomorrow, and tomorrow is the day I make Tamara understand. Today I will make Randolph explain everything to me. He will answer all the questions. It is time he tells me about the first two killings. If he had killed another woman by strangulation like the one he told me about last night, then I have to contact the police and give them all the information I have gathered to date. Then it will be up to them to tie everything together, find all the proof, and send this monster to the gas chamber."

David walked downstairs to the dining room where he knew Randolph would be sitting there, enjoying his morning meal. Just like the past few days, David would join him and pour himself a cup of coffee then take two eggs and three bacon strips off the silver platter. Yeah, it would be much like any of the past four days he had been there. Then it dawned on David. This was Friday. Randolph wouldn't be at breakfast. Randolph had his doctor's appointment this Friday morning. That meant David had heard a car, but where was the dust kicked up by the wheels? There had to be dust. It had not rained in two weeks, so the driveway was dry, and any car driving over that dirt driveway would have had to kick up dust. David had gotten too caught up in the missing dust and had forgotten that each day Randolph had gone to the doctor's, Tamara had not prepared breakfast.

David opened the door to the dining room and walked toward the massive table. Then it hit him. There was no coffee, no eggs, and no bacon waiting for him. He sat down and waited for a few minutes, hoping that Tamara might have heard him enter the room and would bring breakfast in a little bit. He waited for what seemed like hours and heard nothing from the kitchen. He looked down at his watch to discover he had only been waiting for three minutes. "Damn, time passes slowly when you want some coffee." David went to the kitchen, satisfied that Tamara would be there like any other day. But when he opened the door, he found no Tamara, no food waiting. "Shit, no one is here. Well, it looks like you have to fend for yourself, David."

David looked around the kitchen for the coffee, opening each and every cabinet just as empty-handed as he was when he walked into the kitchen. "Damn it! What do I have to do to get some damn coffee?" He continued to search the kitchen for coffee. It wasn't until he had all but given up on his search when he opened the refrigerator, looking for something to eat and came face-to-face with the caffeinated substance of his desire. "*Coffee!* Who in the hell puts coffee in the damn fridge?" David picked up the bag of coffee and set it on the table and turned to the counter where the coffee maker was sitting. He grabbed the glass pot and filled it with cold water from the sink. As he started to pour the water in the coffee maker's reservoir, the door opened behind him.

"What the hell are you doing in my kitchen?" As the words hit David's ears, it caused his hands to turn loose of the glass pot, causing it to fall to the floor and shatter into pieces.

"What the hell. Never enter a room and yell at someone holding a coffee pot. Now look at what you made me do. I can't make coffee now with the pot busted to hell."

"David, don't you ever come into my kitchen without me here again! This is my place, and no one messes with it. Do I make myself clear?"

"Yeah, but what am I to do for coffee now? Wait, you called me David. Don't even try to deny it. You called me David."

"What are you talking about? Why wouldn't I call you David? It is your damn name."

"Yes, it is my name, but you always refer to me as Mr. Erwin. You never call me David."

"I'll call you a damn moronic asshole if you keep standing in my kitchen with that broken glass at your feet. Now for the last time, David, get the hell out of here. I'll make your damn coffee and breakfast as soon as I clean up this mess you've made. Now get the hell out!"

David walked out the door leading to the dining room with one thought running through his head: *She called me David.* He was so distracted he almost walked right overtop of Randolph.

"Watch out, David. You damn near fell all over me. What has your mind so distracted that you couldn't see me sitting here?"

"Well, Randolph, I'm not totally sure which item has the most of my attention, but it would seem something has it. Maybe it is how vague you have been in some areas of the stories you've told me. Maybe it is the last killing you told me about and how her death reminded you of the first killing—a killing you have yet to tell me about. And maybe it is how I can never leave here for even a brief moment without your permission and Justin driving me. Hell, Randolph, maybe it is nothing at all."

"Well, David, I told you from the start that the first two killings would be told to you at the end. I am not ready to disclose those to you yet. Trust that I have good reason for holding them back. As for leaving here, no, I can't let you go off by yourself yet. I would be an affair that you would go straight to the police, and my entire story would never see the light of day. No one will understand me or my art if you were to jump the gun and write these bits and pieces of what was my life. No, I think it best you stay here until the end. It will work out best for us all. If this is not to your liking, I am deeply sorry, but this is how it must be. You agreed to this when you first stepped into my car that dark and dismal night now, didn't you?"

"Yes, Randolph, I guess I did. If I would have known then what I know now, I would have waited until your body appeared on the steps then wrote about that. It might have been more fitting for you than what I might write about now."

"And what might that be, David? What might you write now?"

"Randolph, it is too fucking early in the morning, and I haven't even had my coffee due to you and Tamara being out of the house. So I would highly advise that you refrain from playing your usual games and wait until I have had my *damn* coffee." Just as the words came out of David's mouth, Tamara knocked open the door, nearly knocking it off its hinges, and rushed the breakfast cart over to the table.

"Here's your *damn* coffee, Mr. Erwin. We would not want a guest in this house to be inconvenienced in any way. So please forgive my slacking off and not having your *damn* coffee waiting on you. It wasn't like I had anything else to do. I should have had your coffee waiting in this room, hot and fresh for when you awoke. Yeah, that is what I should have done, if it were not for me having to drive Mr. Cardigan into town because this is Justin's day off. Next time I shall ask Mr. Cardigan to drive himself to his doctor's appointment. Oh yeah, I can't do that. Mr. Cardigan is my employer and he can't drive due to the medication he is on."

After Tamara left the room, the two men looked at each other and shrugged their shoulders as if to ask, "What did I do?"

"David, maybe the next time you're having a bad day, please don't piss off Tamara. She costs me enough money as it is. I really don't want to have to give her another raise to keep her like I did when you first arrived."

"Yes, Randolph, I will do my very best to keep her happy by staying out of her way. I think it is my fault in the first place, and I took my frustrations out on you. I apologize for that, and I will make my apologies known to Tamara once she calms down. Right now, I think it's best I drink my coffee, eat my breakfast, and stay clear of her."

"That would be a great idea, David. Let's both eat and get the hell out of here and over to the study so we limit our access to her right now."

Both men devoured their coffee and breakfast as if they hadn't eaten for weeks. Once finished, they both cleared the room and walked over to the study. "David, you know it might be an hour before Tamara even notices we're not in there anymore."

"Yeah, Randolph. Hell, she might not even peek in there for the next hour, much less go in there. Well, Randolph, you ready to give me the first two murders, or you going to drag this on and on?"

"Well, David, I thought long and hard over telling you about the first two killings and decided it just isn't time yet. So you'll have to wait just a little longer. I know this won't make you happy, but what choice do you have?"

"You're fucking right. I'm not happy! I've been here almost a whole week, and more than once you have made references to the first two killings. Now how the hell can you expect me to write this story of yours without knowing how things began? Never have I heard of a story being told from near the beginning or middle. Okay, whatever, damn it. Let's get this shit over with."

"Now, David, there is no need in cursing and getting upset over something you can't control. I was once like you—impatient, hotheaded, and impetuous. With time and age comes wisdom. So sit back and listen, and you might just learn something about yourself.

"Now where did I leave off? Oh yeah, with sweet Sally's death, it was almost what I needed. However, something was still missing. It just seemed unfulfilling. Nothing like the others I had killed. Sally's death left me wanting more. Usually I would be good for another year or two between killings, but I found myself looking for the next one. I also knew that if I killed someone too close to Sally, there might be something I would leave behind that could connect me to both murders.

"I drove north away from the hotel and farther away from my house. I was thinking that if I could go maybe a hundred or so miles and circle back around away from the area, this would lessen the chance I could be connected to Sally's murder. If I ran across the one person who screamed 'kill me,' then it would appear someone might be on a cross-country killing spree.

"I drove until the sun started to go down and found this little out-of-the-way hotel and stopped for the night. I figured I would sign in under a fake name and pay cash to help ensure I couldn't be connected in any way to Sally's murder. I pulled around the back of the hotel and parked out of the lights. I was trying to make sure no one could see my car and connect it to me or the murder.

"As I was paying the clerk for my room, a young man and his pretty young wife entered the office, and I could overhear them talking. 'John, I don't like this place. Are you sure there isn't a nice place down the road a little ways?'

'Martha, I told you there isn't anything for the next fifty or so miles. I am tired and need to sleep so we can get to your mom's by one p.m. tomorrow. We either stop here or we can sleep in the car. I don't really care which, but you need to make up your mind.'

'I guess you know best, and this will do. But if there are any bugs in the room, I'm leaving.'

"As my arm brushed up against the young lady's arm, that old feeling came sweeping over me. It was like the many times before, the overwhelming hunger. I knew someway, somehow, this young woman would be my next victim. I could almost see it play out in my head. The sweet smell of her blood filling my nostrils, the innocent sounds of her screams rushing through my ears. Oh, what rapture this would be. What fulfillment it would give me.

Nothing like this feeling had overtaken me in such a long time, and I knew I must take this young woman's life.

"The problem I was looking at was how to get her away from her husband. I knew I wouldn't be able to take them both without a struggle. I didn't need the added trouble that came with struggling with two people. This could bring someone running to help or call the police, and then I would be on the run and increase the chances of being caught. This bugged me. Wait, bugs. I remembered hearing the young woman telling her husband that she would leave if she saw any bugs in the room. Now how could I use this to separate the two? And would it even be possible?

"I looked around as I walked to my room for any roaches, ants, spiders, or any bugs I could use. I found three large roaches and scooped them up in this tin can I found lying on the ground. All I needed now was to figure out which room they were in. I walked slowly down the walkway to my room, waiting for them to leave the office and head toward their room. I stood just outside the door of my room, fumbling with the key and door lock as they walked toward me. The young man walked up to the door of the room next to mine. He nodded as if to say hi. I looked clumsily at him and said, 'These locks are never easy to open.'

'Yeah, sometimes they can be a pain.'

'I know. I'm in these flea bags too many times a week. I'm a hardware salesman, and my travels take me to these places all the time. I have yet to find a decent hotel that I would like to stay at more than one time. Well, I've taken up enough yours and your lovely wife's time, and I'm sure you two want to get to bed, so I'll say good night and nice to meet you.'

'Night, sir.'

"I opened the door and walked inside. Like most of the seedy hotels I've stayed at, this being one of the seediest, there was a bed with a flower print bedspread, a nightstand with a lamp, and a small table. The windows were left open to air the room out, I'm guessing. The bathroom was small with half a roll of tissue paper on the roller and one dingy, what used to be white towel on the towel rack. Yeah, this was a real Taj Mahal. Oh well, I would have to make the best of it.

"Just then, I could hear the couple arguing in the room next to me. She was telling him that she didn't want to stay in such a rundown place. How the light didn't work in the bathroom and the room smelled of old dirty socks. Then I heard the door slam shut. I imaged the young woman exiting the room in a huff. I opened the door slowly and peered outside. The young man was standing there, smoking a pipe. The scent of apple hung in the air. He started walking slowly back down to the office to fuss at the desk clerk, I thought. I waited until he was out of sight, then I went out and stood on the sidewalk.

"I lit a cigarette and acted like I was enjoying a smoke in the cool night air. The young man and the desk clerk walked back up the sidewalk. The young man opened the door and let the clerk in. 'Problems with your room?' I asked.

'Yeah, the damn light in the bathroom is out, and my wife is having a fit. I told her there were no other places between here and her mom's house, but she is being pain about it.'

'Well, there is a boarding house here in town. She might be happier with that, but I doubt you will be able to get a room at this hour.'

"Please don't tell my wife. She'll insist on me calling them and making them give us a room. So please don't say anything to her."

'I understand, sir. I won't utter a word about it.' As was finishing my smoke, the desk clerk opened the door.

'Mister, I replaced the light in the bathroom. Will there be anything else?'

'Not that I know of. If my wife is happy, I'm happy.'

The clerk walked back in the direction of the office then stopped mid stride. 'I'm leaving for the rest of the night, so if you do need anything, it will have to wait till morning.' He walked out into the parking lot.

'I guess my wife will have to be happy with the room as it is.'

'With the clerk leaving, she doesn't have much of a choice.'

"John tapped his pipe on the windowsill, and the smoldering embers fell to the sidewalk. 'Night again, sir.'

"You, too, young fella."

"I walked around to the other side of the building, hoping maybe the window might be open. The night air was warm, and with the hotel rooms being a bit warmer, maybe the young couple left a window open. Indeed the window near the bathroom was left slightly opened. I took the tin can that held the three roaches from my jacket pocket and pulled the lid back. I held it up to the window opening, and the roaches slowly made their way into the room. I made my way back to my room unnoticed.

"Now all I would need to do was to wait for the unmistakable screams telling me the young lady would be running out of the room at breakneck speeds. It didn't take nearly as long as I expected before the ear-piercing shrills reached my ears, as high-pitched as any operatic tenor could reach. I opened the door and stepped out on the walkway just as the young lady was rushing out of the room. 'Is everything all right, missy?'

'Hell no. Everything is definitely not all right. There are roaches, cockroaches in my room. I can't abide staying anywhere there are bugs. This is utterly unacceptable. No one should have to put up with this shit.'

'Now, honey, it isn't really as bad as all that.'

'Not that bad, not that bad? Are you staying at the same place I am? Are you out of your freaking mind? I told you I won't stay anyplace that has bugs. Now get off your ass and get our stuff so we can leave!'

'Baby, we can't leave. I've paid for the room, and I am not about to waste the money. We're staying and that's it. Now pull yourself together and stop acting like a baby.'

'Excuse me, sir. Your wife is quite upset, and from what I've heard, she has the right to be. Maybe if you went and talked to the manager and explained the situation to him, he might refund your money.'

'Yeah, he might if he hadn't left. If you remember, he told us that he was leaving after he replaced the light in the bathroom. Even if he were here and did refund my money, where would we stay? I drove all day, and I'm worn out. I can't drive any farther without putting the car into a tree or something.'

'Well, I am not sure, but I think there is another motel up the road about twenty-five miles or so. Do you think you could make it that far safely?'

'Yeah, I can do that, but it better be nicer than here. Hell, if worse, then what will I do? No, we're staying here and that's that. Martha, you need to get over this and grow up.'

'Grow up? How dare you, John.'

"Martha ran off toward the car crying and left John standing there with this blank look on his face. I could just see the light starting to dim in his eyes as he realized he messed up. 'John, you might want to go after her and try to make up. She was hurt by that grow up comment. You might need to get your things and leave. Leaving things as they are with your lovely wife could mean you'll be in the doghouse for a long time.'

'Yeah, you're right. She can be very vindictive when she feels slighted. While I'm packing things up, would you let her know that I'm getting our stuff and will be right there?'

'Yeah, sure thing. I'll make sure she knows, and I'll stay with her to make her feel safe.'

I went over to the young couple's car where she was standing. The whole time I was walking over, I was thinking how to salvage this. What could I do now? I'd just talked them into leaving. I had taken my best opportunity away. I knew that the closest hotel was about one hundred and fifty miles away. I might be able to save this if I followed them. Maybe they would pull off to sleep or something, allowing me to make my move. I had already planned to kill both of them if need be and have a special death for Martha.

'Missy, I talked John into getting y'all things together and heading to the hotel down the road a bit. He should be here in a moment or two. If you don't mind, I'll stay with you until he gets here. You never know what evil could be lurking in the dark these days.'

'Thanks, sir. I'm terribly sorry for the way I acted back there, but I'm not used to low-rent dives like this one. My family is one of means, and to stay somewhere this trashy is just not acceptable. I know that sounds snobbish, but that's how it is.'

'Well, missy, to tell you the truth, this isn't the type of place I stay at most of the time. I'm here for business, and this is all they have here, so I'm sort of stuck.'

'Well, I'm sure John will be here in just a minute, so if you want to go and get some sleep, I'll understand. I know we've kept you up, and I do apologize for that.'

'No need for all that, missy. I'm usually up a bit late anyway. I was preparing for my meeting. And I can't just leave a young lady standing out in the dark by herself. And like you said, John will be here soon.'

'Thanks again, mister.'

"Just then, John walked up and unlocked the car."

'Sir, thanks again for waiting here with my wife. Let me make it up to you in some way. This whole ordeal must have been quite taxing for you.'

"John reached out his hand as if to shake mine, so I stretched out mine. As we shook hands, I felt something hiding in Johns' palm. When I pulled my hand back, I looked down and saw a crumpled-up paper. I started to uncrumple it and noticed that it was money. John had handed me two hundred-dollar bills, and before I could say anything, John interrupted me.

'No, you must take it. We have intruded on you and your sleep enough. This is the least we can.'

'John, this isn't necessary. You and your lovely wife haven't kept me up. Like I told Martha, I was up preparing for my meeting anyway.'

'In that case, please take this as well.'

"John handed me his business card and told me to call him in a few days to discuss my business."

'I'm always looking for something that can help my company, and who knows, you may have something we need.'

'Well, John, I never pass up an opportunity. I'll call you on Monday around one p.m.'

'That will be perfect.'

'I'd offer my card, but it seems I left without any.'

"That's okay. I'm glad we had a chance to meet and that you were here to help look after my wife. Again, thanks so much.'

"John and his wife pulled off, and I quickly walked back to my room and locked the door. I got in the car and pulled off after them. It wasn't long until I caught up with them. I left my lights off so they wouldn't see me yet. We drove for about twenty-five miles, and their car stared to weave. I could tell John was starting to fall asleep. I just needed to wait a bit longer. He would nod off and, with a bit of luck, drive off the road into the trees. With John driving slowly, I was certain they wouldn't get hurt.

"We went about another ten miles or so, then their car started weaving again. This time it went right off the road and into a stand of trees just off the right side of the road. I saw the car come to an abrupt stop and heard it collide with a tree. I pulled off the road, got out, and walked down the hill toward their car. I couldn't see if anyone was moving around, so I crept up quietly.

"When I got just a few feet from the car, I could see a silhouette of the passenger moving. If John was unconscious, I didn't want Martha to wake him. I ran up and grabbed the door handle. I flung open the passenger side door, and Martha was sitting there with blood running down her face from a small gash on her forehead. I reached in and pulled her out of the seat.

"John was laying slumped over the steering wheel, out cold. I led Martha to the stand of trees and set her down. 'My husband, my husband, he's still in the car!' Martha shouted. I couldn't afford to have John wake up and interrupt me.

'Ma'am, I'll get your husband. Wait here.' I went back to the car and over to the driver's side. John was still slumped over the wheel and out cold. I checked to make sure he was still breathing. Just barely, but breathing he was. I walked back over to Martha. 'Ma'am, I'm sorry, but your husband didn't make it.'

'No, no!' she cried out.

'Come with me, ma'am. I have a place right past the tree. There I can see to your wounds and send for the sheriff. He'll see to your husband.'

"It was dark enough that she couldn't make out who it was talking to her. She held out her hand, and I helped her to her feet. We walked into the woods, and when I felt we were far enough away from the road, we stopped. 'Here, ma'am, sit here and rest for a few.' I helped her to a nearby tree, and she slumped to the ground.

'Are you sure John is dead? Are you sure? Please tell me you are mistaken and he is not dead. Please tell me he isn't dead!'

'No, ma'am. He isn't dead. He's just unconscious, but soon you will be dead.' She paused for a second in disbelief. I reached into my pocket and pulled out my pocketknife. Then she started to cry again.

'Kill me? You're going to kill me? That's fine. I don't want to live without my husband anyway, so go ahead and kill me.'

'John is still very much alive. I left him still slumped over the steering wheel like I found him. He'll be out for a few hours, but he is still alive.'

'You called him John. How do you know us? What did we do to you?'

'You and John met me back at the hotel, remember?'

'You're the nice man that waited by the car with me and was staying in the room next to ours.'

'Yes, ma'am. See, I'm out here on business. I was out this way looking for the one person who could fulfill my hunger for blood and my zest for killing, and you are that person. You and your husband have done nothing to me, nor would that matter. You were just in the wrong place at the wrong time. Much like all the others I have killed.'

"She cried out, 'John, John, help me please.' I grabbed her by the hair and drew my knife closer to her.

"After I finished with Martha, I drove back to the hotel. I made sure to pull around back again to minimize the chances of waking someone up and them seeing my car. I parked and made my way back into my room and laid down on the bed. My heart was pumping hard and fast. The excitement was overwhelming.

"I had just killed a woman not more than a hundred yards from where her unconscious husband was and left him alive. I thought about killing him as well, but it just didn't fit. The hunger was gone once Martha took her last breath. So why kill him? I didn't need him.

"As the bright morning sun broke through the window and woke me, I heard a knock on the door. 'Just a minute!' I shouted. I put my clothes on and opened the door. Standing there was the clerk from the front desk last night.

'Mister, did you see the people in the room next to yours leave last night?'

'Yes. The young lady said she saw roaches in their room and wasn't staying a second longer. They argued for a few minutes, then her husband went into the room to get their things. I waited by their car with the lady to make sure she felt safe, then they left.'

'Well, they forgot to sign the register last night, and they left a bag in their room. Maybe they'll come back and get their bag. Thanks again, sir, and I'm sorry for bothering you.' The clerk left, and I shut the door. I gathered my things, went to my car, and drove around to the front of the hotel to check out.

"I drove out to where I left John and his wife. The sheriff's car was parked on the side of the road where John's car had swerved off. I pulled off right behind the sheriff's car and got out. A tall man was standing there in a brownish colored uniform, looking around. I walked up and asked if everything was okay.

'Well, sir, there's a car off in the woods over there. I was about to see what's going on.'

'Is there anything I can do to help?'

'Right now, there's nothing to be done. I'll check on the driver and go from there.' The deputy walked down the hill to John's car and opened the door. He yelled back, 'There's a man here unconscious!' I walked down to the car and said, 'I think I know the car, Officer.'

'Yeah, who is it? Do know this fellow here?'

'Yes, sir, I do. Well, kind of. I met him and his wife last night at this hotel I stayed at. They left because she found roaches in their room. I don't really know them other than that. His name is John, and his wife's is Martha.'

'John, are you all right?" the deputy shouted. 'John where's your wife?' John started to move and straighten up in his seat. He placed his hand on the shifter to help steady himself. He removed his hand and looked down at it, sort of puzzled. There was blood dripping from John's hand.

'Sir, are you all right?'

'I think so.' John was still looking at his hand, then he leaned back into the seat and looked down at the gear shifter and screamed, 'Oh my god! Oh my god!'

"The sheriff looked into the car and backed up as he was pulling John from the car.

'There's a human heart stuck on the shifter. Will you stay with this man while I call this in?'

'Yes, sir, of course. I'll stay with him.'

"John was yelling out, 'Martha! Martha! Where is my wife? Oh god, where is Martha?'

'John, this is Randolph. We met last night. Do you remember me or what happened after you left the hotel? We'll find Martha, John. We'll find her.'

"The deputy walked back up to us. 'They'll be ten officers here in a few minutes, sir, and we'll start looking for your wife. But for now, I need you to tell me what happened here. Can you do that, sir? Can you do that?'

'Where's Martha? Where's my wife?'

'Sir, I need you to talk to me. I need you to tell me what happened here. What happened to your wife? Whose heart is that? Where did it come from?'

'I don't know. I don't know. Where's my wife? Where's Martha? Oh god, where's Martha?'

'Sir, please. I need you to calm down. We can't do anything unless you can tell us what happened here.'

"John was crying frantically, and the deputy was getting nowhere. 'Let me see if I can get through to him, Officer.'

'Okay, give it a try and see what you can find out.'

'John,' I said. 'You need to calm down and try to remember what happened last night after you and Martha left the hotel. Can you do that for me, John?'

'Yes, I think so, but where's my Martha?'

'John, we need you to tell us what happened. This deputy is going to ask you some questions so that we can find Martha. You need to try and answer him as best you can. Can you do that, John?'

"I shook John a little in hopes that might bring him around so the officer could talk to him. 'Okay, okay. I'll do my best. Stop shaking me.'

'Sir, I'm Deputy Jackson. Can you tell me what happened last night after you and your wife left the hotel?'

'Well, sir, I drove out looking for another hotel, and I guess I fell asleep and drove off into this tree. After that, I don't know anything until I woke up here and saw all that blood on my hand. Then I saw the heart stuck there. Where's Martha? We need to go look for her. She's probably scared out of her mind. When can we start looking for my Martha?'

'Sir, we'll look for your wife, but you need to stay here. There's an ambulance on its way here, and the EMTs will look you over. But for now, let's go over this again. The better I know what happened, the better the chances are we will be able to find your wife. So you and your wife left the hotel where you were at in search of another hotel. Why did you and your wife leave that hotel, sir?'

'We left because my wife found cockroaches in our room and

she can't stand bugs. We don't usually stay in places like that, but I was tired and was afraid I might fall asleep while driving, so we stopped there. Martha didn't like it from the start and was complaining the entire time we were there. This man was nice enough to stay by the car with my wife while I got our bags and we could leave. Hell, he talked me into leaving there anyway.'

'What's your name, sir, and is it true you talked them into leaving?'

'I'm Randolph Cardigan, and I guess in a way it is true, sir. His wife was so frantic about the bugs that she wasn't about to go back into the room. I told this young fellow that it might be best if they went on, and I thought there might be another hotel down the road a few miles. So, yeah, I guess I did talk him into leaving.'

'Was there any other reason you wanted them to leave, Mr. Cardigan?'

'Other than to get some sleep, no, sir. It looked to me like his wife wasn't going to go back into the room, and it might be better for them to find somewhere else to stay than for her to sleep in their car.'

'Is this true, John? He told you that there might be another hotel down the road, and you decided to leave to please your wife?'

'Yes, that's true, sir. Now can we search for my Martha?'

'In a minute, John. I still have a few questions, and we need to wait for the other officers to show up and help us search. Now, John, I need you to think hard. Do you remember if anyone was following you? Did you see any other cars?'

'No, sir. We were alone on the road. I don't remember seeing any cars either behind us or coming from the other directions.'

'Mr. Cardigan, were you at your hotel room the whole night?'

'Yes, sir. I was there and asleep in my room until the desk clerk woke me this morning.'

'Why did the clerk wake you up?'

'He asked me if the young man and his wife left during the night. I told him that the young lady found roaches in the room and didn't want to stay there so they left. He found the door to their room open but they weren't there, and they had left a bag behind. After he left, I got dressed and left.'

'Why were you at this hotel, sir?'

'I stopped there on my way to a meeting that I was supposed to be at in ten minutes. I was looking at a local newspaper that I might buy if the price is right.'

'Are you a reporter?'

'Well, no, sir. I own a few papers, and I was looking to buy another one.'

'Well, just in case, I'm going to have to ask you not to write about this until his wife is found. If someone took her, they might be waiting to see this in a newspaper; and we don't want to let them know we know anything yet. Do I have your word that this won't be in your papers until his wife is found?'

'Absolutely, sir. I won't do anything to hinder your efforts in finding this poor man's wife. When can we start looking for her? Can I help?'

"We'll need all the eyes we can get, but we can't start till the other officers get here."

It wasn't long till, "Wait just a damn second."

"What is it, David? I am trying to get this told before I go to bed, and I can't do that if you're going to interrupt me. So what is it, David?"

"You sick fuck. You joined the search for the woman you killed. How fucked up is that? You took the chance of being caught to make sure your handiwork was found."

"David, what better way to throw off suspicion than to be right in front of their noses? Now do you mind if I finish this and get to bed?

"Now where was I? Oh, yeah. Right about then, the ambulance and a few sheriff cars pulled up. The EMTs looked over John, and Deputy Jackson started telling the other officers what was going.

'Now, guys, what we have here is a husband and wife that ran their car off the road, and the wife most likely wandered off. She is probably hurt and confused. I want you guys to pair up and make a circle around the car. Then start walking outward away from the car when you can't see either team beside you, then the two men split off. This will cover the most amount of area in the shortest time. Now let's get to it. When someone finds the missing woman, yell out, then meet everyone back at the car.'

'Excuse me, Officer, but can I help?'

'Mr. Cardigan, you can best help us by staying here out of the way and keeping John calm. We don't want you to accidentally mess up evidence that might be out there. Everyone ready?' asked the deputy. 'Now let's start. If you run across anything, yell out and I'll be right there.'

"The officers started fanning out, and Deputy Jackson was with another officer heading in the direction where I left Martha lying. I knew it wouldn't be long before the two men would find her and come running. I went over to the ambulance to stay with John while the officers searched.

'John, the officers are looking for Martha now, and I'm sure they'll find her.'

'I hope she's all right. She is quite the fragile thing.'

'I'm sure she just wandered off, confused, and is waiting somewhere close by.'

'You really think she's all right? You really think so?'

"Suddenly a scream screeched through the forest. 'What's that? Who screamed?'

'John, now don't panic. It's probably just someone who walked up on a snake.'

"Deputy Jackson came running past me with a terrified look on his face. He looked as if he had just seen the scariest thing imaginable. 'Deputy Jackson, is everything okay?'

"He waved his hand at the EMT and motioned him over. I told John to stay there, and I would find out what's going on. I followed the EMT over to the deputy.

'Is everything all right, Steve?' asked the EMT.

'Get your bag and follow me,' said Deputy Jackson. The EMT went back to the ambulance and grabbed a small black bag.

'Deputy, is everything okay? Have you found John's wife? Is she hurt? What can I tell John, if anything?'

'Mr. Cardigan, right now don't tell him anything. What I saw was the most terrifying and disturbing sight I've ever seen.'

'What did you see?'

'She didn't have a face. She didn't have a face. It has to be his wife, but there is no face.'

'Well, I remember what she was wearing, I think. Do you want me to come with you and identify her if I can?'

'Sir, I wouldn't ask anyone to view what I just saw, but if you're willing to try and ID what's left, then follow me, sir. But let me forewarn you, this sight is very gruesome and made me and Deputy Samuel sick.'

'Deputy, do I need to bring anything other than my bag?' asked the EMT.

'Shush,' said Deputy Jackson. He then made some sort of motion to the EMT like he was trying to fold something. The EMT went back to the ambulance and came back to where the deputy and I were standing. 'I got a clean sheet as you directed, Steve. I take it you found her, but she ain't alive.'

'Damn it, Burt, keep your voice down. I don't want to upset her husband yet. Just follow me and do your damn job.'

'Okay, Steve, okay.'

"Deputy Jackson led me and the EMT back to where the body was. I though the EMT would never stop vomiting after he laid eyes on Martha's body. She was still sitting there, propped up against the tree where I had left her.

'What kind of animal could have done this, to eat her face off like that?' asked the EMT.

'The two-legged type, Burt, the two-legged type. Her face wasn't eaten. She was skinned.'

'No way, Steve. You mean someone took time to do this to her?'

"Martha was sitting there without a face. There was a hole in her chest where her heart used to be, and I had left her face lying on the ground under her legs so animals would take off with it. The facial muscles were still slightly wet with the blood that poured out of the veins connected to what used to be her face. I had even cut her nose and lips off so I didn't ruin the complete beauty of her face.

"Sitting there looking forward with bare eyes and no lids to cover them, her shirt was soaked red in her blood, not from the hole in her chest but rather from the skinning she withstood. I wouldn't have had to cut her heart out if she would have died from removing her face. No, she was much stronger than I thought she was. I just couldn't leave her there, screaming in pain, and simply cutting her throat or stabbing her wouldn't do. No, I had to do something special. Something that would make her stand out, something that said I enjoyed taking my time with her.

"Leaving her sitting there with her shirt closed and the only thing that even told someone to look behind her shirt was the fact that where one side bulged out and the other didn't. When the EMT opened her blouse, he started vomiting again. Damn, this motherfucker had the weakest constitution I'd ever seen. The deputy bent over to get a closer look and quickly stepped back and joined the EMT in tandem vomiting.

"For the first time, I got to see my handiwork in the daylight. Martha's breast was lying under her arm. I had cut it and skinned it back enough to reveal her ribcage. All that was left was the few muscles and ribs still oozing and dripping blood. I went back to my car and got a hammer from the truck. I had used the hammer to break through the ribs to her heart. Did you know that each rib makes a different sound when struck by a steel hammer? Would you believe she stayed alive right up until I cut her heart out. Damn, she was strong-willed. She wanted to live more than any other I had killed. I have never come across anyone with a will to match Martha's. She will always have a special place in my heart. Ha ha ha. A pun. Even now I can make jokes."

"Randolph, you are one sick fuck. That is all I can say. I remember something about that story. Wasn't the husband convicted for her murder? Didn't they find enough evidence to nail a conviction?"

"Yes, they did. I must say it is pretty easy to get fingerprints on a bloody hammer when the prints belong to someone unconscious. They found the hammer about fifty feet from her body with his prints in the blood. The hammer matched one he was known to keep in his truck. You know, what a stroke of luck that was. I didn't have to buy another hammer. Well, time for bed. I'll see you around one p.m. tomorrow afternoon."

"Are you going out again in the morning? Well, I think I'll go ask Tamara if there happens to be any of that delicious pie left."

"Don't bother. She asked for the night off, and I told her she could as long as she was back here for breakfast. Night, David."

"Good night, Randolph. I guess I'll head on to bed, too."

Tamara had asked for the night off so she could get away from the house and David for a while. She found herself walking down Bourbon Street in New Orleans. She walked into Pat O'Brien's and took a seat at the bar.

"Hi, Tamara. It's been a long time since I've seen you in here," said the man behind the bar.

"Hi, Jamie. Yeah, I've been busy and haven't been able to get by."

"The usual?"

"Yeah, why mess with perfection?"

The barkeep went over to a machine with a glass cover and pulled the black handle. A cold blue slushy concoction slowly oozed into the tall plastic container.

"One Hurricane coming up. Are you still working out there at the old house?"

"Yeah, I'm still there."

"Why don't you take your education and find something better than playing housekeep to some old fart?"

"That old fart pays me more than I can get at some office job. Plus, I can't stand the thought of working for corporate America anymore. Always having to worry about profit margins, sales reports. Not to mention all the other bullshit that goes along with that day-to-day grind called the nine-to-five. No thanks. I think I'll stay right where I am."

Tamara didn't notice that someone had walked up and sat down at the bar a few seats down from her.

"Nine-to-five grind, huh. Yeah, I'm glad that ain't me. I couldn't see me behind a desk pushing pencils and shuffling papers. I'll stick to my truck, thanks. Hey, barkeep, can I get a beer please?"

"Sure thing, sir. Right away."

"And what gives you the right to butt into our conversation?"

"Well, I didn't mean to butt in, but from where I was sitting, it sounded like you were done with your dissertation. So I put my two cents in. I'm sorry if it wasn't welcomed, but hey, that's me."

"No, sir, it wasn't welcome, nor was it wanted."

"Well, la de da and forgive me. I'll just sit here and drink my beer alone just like you are drinking your blue drink, alone and by yourself. Just two people drinking alone in a crowded bar on a Friday night. Yep, two lonely people in a crowded bar on a Friday night."

Tamara laughed under her breath. "Was that a laugh I heard? Did I say something to break through that hard exterior of yours?"

"Yeah, that was a laugh. Lonely and alone on a Friday night in a crowded bar. I've spent too many Friday nights alone in this place, so I guess it won't kill me to share a lonely night just this once."

The man moved over a few seats closer to Tamara and asked, "What's that blue mess called anyway?"

"It's a Hurricane. It's the signature drink here, and it's quite delicious. You should try it."

"No, thanks. I make it a habit not to drink anything blue. It reminds me of something else that gets blue from time to time."

"And what might that be, sir?"

"Well, little lady, if you need to ask, you might not be old enough to be in this bar."

Again Tamara laughed. This time she didn't try to hold it back. "Now that's better. A laugh and not a snicker."

"Thank you, sir. I needed a good laugh."

"Well, stick around and maybe I can do that again."

"Maybe I will stick around for a bit. At least until I've finished my drink."

He was a few years older than her, but she didn't mind the age difference. He was bald and wearing a cowboy hat. "Excuse me, sir, but that beer is $2.75. If you give a credit card, I can run you a tab."

"Well, I ain't sure if I'll be here long enough to run a tab. Well, if this pretty lady is going to be and will allow me to buy her a drink, then I'll run a tab."

"Was that your cute way of asking if you could buy me a drink?"

"Only if it worked. But if not, then I guess it wasn't cute enough."

"Well, all right, but don't think I come here for some man to sweep me off my feet and into his bed. I'm more than capable of buying my own drinks and yours, too. But that was cute, so go ahead and buy one for now."

"You heard the lady, barkeep. Set us up again and run that tab please." The stranger handed the bartender his credit card.

"Thanks, sir. Here's your card back. Just let me know when you need something. Ma'am, if he gets out of hand, I'll be right over here."

"I'll be fine, James. Anyways, he looks pretty harmless."

"Well, missy, what brings a pretty little thing like you in here tonight? By the way, my friends call me JJ."

"Nice to meet you, JJ. I'm Tamara. I come here every now and again, but tonight I just needed to get away from work for a while. Since we're playing twenty questions, what brings you in here?"

"Well, I am stuck here for the next thirty-six hours doing a restart, and I didn't much feel like spending it in my truck again."

"I see. You're a truck driver. Do you drive all over or locally? Scratch that, locally thing. Seeing how you're stuck here, you can't be a local driver."

"No, ma'am. I'm not. I drive all the lower forty-eight states and parts of Canada."

"Are you married? Being a truck driver must be hard on your home life."

"No, I'm not married. And yes, it can be very hard on someone's home life. What type of work do you do?"

"I work as a housekeeper for well-off elderly gentleman. I do the cooking, cleaning, bill paying, and just about anything else he needs done."

"Hum, just about anything else. That's a broad list of things to get done. I hope he pays you well."

"Yes, he pays me very well. However, the last few days he's had this man staying there, and he's getting under my skin."

"How so? What's he been doing to get you so riled up, if you don't mind me asking?"

"He's just a pig. You know a pig, like most men are. They think we women are put here for their pleasure and not much else. Wait a second. What did you mean by that comment you made?"

"What comment?"

"Don't do that. Don't play it off like you don't know what I'm talking about. Give me some credit for having half a brain at least."

"I assure you I don't know what comment you're referring to, but if you tell me, I'll be happy to tell you what I meant."

"I'm sure you will. I'm even more certain that you will play it off as if you didn't mean anything by it as if I'm just some dumb female waiting to open her legs for a charmer like you. So it's best if you just admit to it now and we can move on and get it out of the way."

"Tamara, I'd love to tell you I know what you're talking about. but I don't have the foggiest. If you feel that I've said or done something to offend you, tell me what it is. I'll gladly explain myself and apologize for the offense."

"My ass. You know damn well what you said. Why should I justify you by repeating it? Where do you get off talking to me in that manner?"

"Barkeep."

"Yes, sir," asked James.

"Two things. One, my tab please. And two, tell this lady she's out of her mind. I was just hoping for some nice conversation with a pretty lady who looked like she might need someone to listen to her. Then she went off her meds or something and started hounding me about a comment I made that I have no clue about, and she refuses to enlighten me. So let's close out my tab and I'll call it a night."

"Wait just a damn minute, baldy. You know damn good and well what you said. Now before you tuck tail and run, admit to it and maybe I'll forget about it."

James handed JJ his receipt and waited for him to sign it.

"Forget about it. Hell, I'm sure you will remind me of whatever it is from now till hell freezes over. Again, ma'am, I have no fucking clue what you think you heard, and at this point I really don't give a fuck. So if you don't mind, shut the hell up and leave me alone as I am sure to leave you be."

JJ signed the small piece of paper, grabbed his hat. and started walking toward the door.

"What the fuck. You're just going to walk out without apologizing. Some gentleman you turned out to be."

"Lady, I really don't give a shit what you think or say at this point. As for an apology, I'm not in the practice of apologizing for shit I have no damn clue about. Now good night and go fuck yourself."

JJ walked out the door, and the people still in there could hear the door slam against the solid wooden jamb. He slammed it so hard the bartender had to walk over and take a look to make sure JJ didn't damage it.

"Well, the nerve of some people. James, why do you let men like him in here?"

"Tamara, I didn't know he would upset you so much. By the way, what did he say to you?"

"Well, he asked what I did for a living; and I told him I work as a housekeeper for well-off elderly gentleman. I do the cooking, cleaning, bill paying, and just about anything else he needs done. Then he said, 'Hum, just about anything else.' Now I ask you, was that comment what I think it was? Was he accusing me of sleeping with my employer?"

"Well, ma'am, I'm not sure. He could have just been playing and didn't mean anything by it. You might have misunderstood the meaning or misheard it. Hell, Tamara, it could have been damn near anything."

"Bullshit! He said what he said and now you're defending him. More bullshit. Good night, James."

Tamara walked out the door in a huff and slammed it behind her. Then she opened it again and slammed it again.

"Damn feminists. They always blow shit way out of proportion." James went back to washing the glasses. Tamara walked down the street a few feet and turned back to the bar.

"No! I'll be damned if I'll be talked to like that. Hell, I didn't need to leave Mr. Cardigan's for this shit. I could have stayed there and got the same crap from David." She walked back to her car and drove off.

David laid there in his bed, thinking of what to say to Tamara. How could he possibly convince her he loves her, and it wasn't just some scheme to get into her pants? "Damn it, if I hadn't been my normal self from the start. If only I had stopped myself from opening my mouth and placing my foot squarely inside. Well, not much I can do about the past. I have to figure out how to convince her that I am sincere. I know this much. I can't come across as some lovesick fool."

David nodded off with one thought lodged in his brain: how to win Tamara and how to make her understand that he's not the same prick that walked through those doors almost a week ago. As David drifted off to sleep, the familiar black car pulled in front of the house. Tamara stepped out. Justin met her at the front door. "You're home earlier than expected."

"Yeah, Justin. I didn't expect to be home this early, either. Is everyone tucked into bed?"

"Yes, ma'am. Mr. Cardigan and his guest went off to bed two hours ago."

"Good. Then things should be quiet and I might be able to get some work done. Night, Justin."

"Good night, ma'am."

Justin got in the car and drove off. "I don't see why Mr. Cardigan has Justin take the car into town each night. That doesn't make sense. Why not just leave it here locked up? I'm sure, by now, David wouldn't try to steal it and run off. But why has Justin been ordered not to come to the house tomorrow? For crap's sake, I don't understand most of the shit Randolph does. I've been here for three years and I've received six raises in that time. This just ain't normal. Normal...nothing that man does is normal."

Tamara walked into the kitchen where the dinner dishes were still waiting for her. "Damn, I knew I shouldn't have left without cleaning this mess up." As she started cleaning up the after the evening's meal, her mind started wandering. Her thoughts were betraying her, leading her to daydream of David, dreams of things she wanted the hear him say. She so desperately needed him to say how much she meant to him, how much he loved her.

"How could you let yourself do this? How could you allow an utter pig get inside you so deeply? How was he able to penetrate the cold iron security you worked so hard to put in place? Tamara, you fool, you know love is for the foolhardy. It's just a fictional emotion weak-minded people allow to rule their lives." The harder she cleaned, the more vivid the daydreams became. With every passing second, her heart beat faster and faster. Her blood was rushing through her veins, screaming for David. "This cannot be. I can't be in love with him. Not him. Never him." More and more she tried to deny the feelings flooding her soul. With every beat of her heart, the feeling grew stronger.

"Get hold of yourself, Tamara. You're not some lovesick schoolgirl. Put this foolish notion out of your head. You know there could never be anything in your life for David." As she stood there, she noticed that all the work was done. She couldn't even remember washing the dishes, putting them away, or cleaning anything. Her thoughts of David had so completely overtaken her, she knew of nothing else. Everything around her had vanished. Nothing existed, not her work, not the house, nothing.

"How can this be? I never allow anything to take my mind off my work. What is it about this pig, this womanizing pile of dog crap? Yeah, girl, keep telling yourself he is all that. He is the epitome of all the horrid things you find distasteful in men. He's the evil you've been avoiding all your life. Yeah, keep telling yourself all that and more, and maybe you'll start believing it." With all her work finished and nothing else to do to try and keep her mind off David, she walked up to her bedroom. As she was passing the door leading into David's room, she stopped and passed, listening for the faintest sounds of life. She was hoping he was still awake, wishing he would come out and take her into his arms.

As she slowly opened the door to her room, she looked back down the hall at the door to David's room. "It would be so easy to just walk in and take what I want. To make him understand how madly in love with him I am. What if you do that, girl? What if you did and he took what he wanted and left you with nothing? Told you that you're just a passing fancy, a piece of ass. Then what? You would be devastated, destroyed beyond anything you have ever known."

As the door shut behind her and she found herself alone in her room, those feelings for David grew stronger yet. As she was taking her clothes off and standing there with her soft silky breasts shimmering in the light, she wished David was there touching her, squeezing her breasts, kissing her lips, caressing every inch of her body, bringing her to the erotic explosion she so desired. She lay back on her bed and allowed her thoughts of David to wash over her like the warm water of a steamy shower.

The daydream of the ecstasy she desired wasn't enough. This could never take the place of what lay waiting for her behind the closed door down the hall. "Girl, you're stupid if you think you're going down there just so you can be his plaything for the night. He'll use and throw you away like some trash waiting for the weekly garbage pickup. He'll leave you shattered and broken, and then what will become of you? Can you see yourself chasing after him like some whipped lovestruck teenager? Get real, girl. This ain't you. You're better than this." She kept trying to talk herself out of the one compelling, overwhelming thought that had started to consume her. She mustn't allow herself to do what she was driving herself to do. She couldn't allow David to win.

As David lay sleeping, slowly the door opened to his room. Tamara was careful not to make a sound. She didn't want to wake him until she was ready. She stepped softly into the room and closed the door behind, taking extra care to ensure it made no sounds as it mated with the doorjamb and latched tight. She stepped in, one foot at a time, gently. Each foot caressed the floor as she made her way to David's bed.

What are you doing? You know he will just throw you away when he's done with you. Oh well, if he does, he does, at least I'll have tonight. At least he will be mine for a brief moment in time. Until he does throw me away like some old used rag, I would have had this night. Now shut the fuck up, self, and let's enjoy what we came here for.

Tamara stood there, looming over the bed where David lay sleeping. Looking down, she thought how sweet he looked. *How could someone that looks so sweet hurt me? He's like sugar candy to a child, and I'm that child tonight.* She leaned over David and slowly drew her face closer to his. Her hot steamy breath bounced back off David's face, the sound of her heart thundering in her ears.

She bent lower and lower until her lips were a heartbeat away from touching David's. *Now, girl, be gentle. If you go in too strong, it will startle him and ruin everything.* Her lips barely touched his and she backed away. *What are you doing? Get to it already. We don't have all night.* With her courage waning, she wasn't sure she could go through with this. She would make one more attempt, and if she stopped again, she would go back to her room and forget she was ever here.

David was awoken with tender loving lips meeting his. He reached out and gently pulled Tamara to him. He couldn't believe she was here with him. She had come to him, and he could now tell her the little words that had filled his heart and soul. "I love you, Tamara. I love you with all that I am."

"David, please don't toy with my feelings. Please allow this to be real. I have never allowed anyone in as deeply as you. It would crush me if this wasn't real, so please let this be real, even if for only this moment."

"Oh, Tamara, this is more real than you know. I've been trying to work up the courage to come to you and make you understand how I feel. I was so terrified you would turn me away. So filled with dread of not being able to show you the true me—what you have brought out in me. I'm not the man I was when I entered this house, nor will I be that man ever again. It's all because of you."

"Shush. Let tonight be ours. No words, no chances to screw

this up. Let's just be with each other. Hold me close and never let me go. Do this for me tonight, and we'll see what tomorrow will bring."

David wrapped his arms around her gently, as not to break her. He wanted so much to hold Tamara for eternity. She felt the strength and tenderness hidden within David's touch. Tamara hadn't known anything like this. She never knew love could be so soft and tender, yet strong and never yielding. She was allowing herself to let go for the first time in her life.

Their bodies lay there in the entangled and blissful embrace only known by the gods. No other human could ever feel the way these two lovers felt. David's touch brought her to the heights that she was always denied. She was never able to experience the ecstasy brought to her by David's hands. David had never known that something he once considered as a conquest could be something so beautiful, so tender, and so loving. The two lovers spent the rest of the night lost in each other's embrace. Nothing existed. Time itself stopped; and for that moment, only they existed.

David awoke in the morning to the familiar smell of bacon and coffee. He turned to look beside him for his sweet Tamara, only to find the space beside him empty. *Was it just a cruel dream? Did my subconscious concoct it to fool me? Could I be that cruel to myself?* These questions ran through David's mind as he lay there.

"I can't see her just yet. Not as long as the vividness of that dream lurks in my mind. I'll stay here until breakfast is over, then I won't have to face her and try to hide what's inside of me." David rose from his bed and went into the washroom and washed his face. He didn't hear the door to his room open and close. As he walked back into the bedroom, he was face-to-face with Tamara, standing there and holding a tray of coffee, bacon, eggs, and toast.

"What's this? Breakfast in bed brought to me by the most beautiful apparition I could possible imagine."

"Apparition I am not, dear sir," Tamara said as she stood there holding the tray of food with nothing but a smile. "Would an apparition bring you coffee in the nude? Would it be waiting for you while you washed the sleep from your eyes?"

"No, I am certain of that. No apparition I could dream up would wake me during the night and take me to heights I could never find on my own. Nor would one so beautiful bring me coffee, so you cannot be an apparition, my sweet love. You have to be real. There can be no other conclusion."

"Real I am, dear David. Real I am. If not for you, I would have gone the rest of my life without knowing what love felt like. If there is nothing more for you and I, at least I learned that, and I experienced one night of majestic passion I never knew could exist. Come lie down and allow me to serve you as you deserve to be served."

"No, Tamara. You shall never be a servant to me. I shall forever be yours." David took the tray from Tamara and led her to the bed. He guided her to lie down and pulled the covers up over her. "Now, my lady, allow me to serve you breakfast in bed." David pulled the legs of the tray out and locked them in place and placed the tray over Tamara's lap. David then walked around to the other side and slid under the cover to join her.

"David, was last night real? Did you really say those things to me? Were they just words to ensure you got what you wanted? Please tell me. I need to know it was real."

Tamara lifted the cup to her lips and took a sip of the dark liquid held inside.

"Tamara, nothing could ever be as real as last night. I could never have meant anything more than I meant the words I spoke to you. I've been waiting, hunting for the right time to approach you and try to make you understand how much you changed me. How much I love you, how desperately I need you. So no, my love, it wasn't a dream. It was very real indeed. But I have to ask, why did you come to my room this morning nude? And didn't Randolph see you?"

"No, he never saw me," she said as she laughed. "He never comes down for breakfast on Saturdays. He has usually left by now and doesn't return until one in the afternoon. As for being nude, I thought I would give you a choice for your morning delight. To my surprise, you turned the tables on me and did something totally selfless and considerate. You didn't think of yourself at all. You thought of me first. I have never had anyone serve me breakfast in bed, much less put me first."

"My love, you will always be first in my life, and I shall forever be your servant."

The two lovestruck lovers sat there for a few minutes, then Tamara picked up a piece of bacon and fed it to David. "Well, I know this much. I didn't make this for it to go to waste, so I guess we'll share it and I'll just have to feed you. As for servant, I think not. Maybe we will be servants to each other to keep things fair."

David bit down on the bacon and then nibbled a bit on Tamara's neck. "Now hold right there, sir. We eat the food before it gets cold, then you and I can nibble on each other."

"Where does Randolph go on Saturdays? I know most doctor's offices are closed on the weekends."

"I'm not sure. He has never told me, and I asked him once. He only muttered something about time being short and things needed done."

"Hmm, I wonder what he meant by that. Maybe he was referring to his own life coming to an end and him needing to put his affairs in order before he dies."

"Yeah, it's got to be something like that. Why are we laying here in this bed and I'm naked and you're not and we're talking about Randolph? What's wrong with that picture, dear David?"

"Yes, ma'am, I get the hint." David stood up and removed his clothes and started to get back under the covers.

"Wait just a second, mister. I didn't get to see what I was buying last night. I want to get my eyes full and my money's worth, so just hold on a minute." Tamara sat there, looking over every inch of David's body, licking her lips as her eyes moved up and down. David turned slightly to the left and then to the right as if he was modeling for an advertisement.

They both broke out in laughter as David climbed back under the covers alongside his loving Tamara. "David, have you ever had a fantasy? You know, something you wanted to do or try but was never comfortable letting anyone know for fear they'd make fun or wouldn't understand. Have you ever had something like that?"

"The only thing I have been able to think about the past few days is you. The only fantasies I have had are filled with you, and you fulfilled them last night by coming into my room. Up until then, I have never had any type of fantasy. I had always thought sex was sex."

"What about now? Is it still just sex for you?"

"Hell no! I found something last night I never knew existed. I found you. What I experienced with you last night was so much more than sex could ever be. I found someone who wants and loves me, someone who could see past the bullshit I was putting off and see the real me. The me that needed to be loved and needed to love someone. You, my dear sweet Tamara, brought the word to a new light for me. I could never go back to being the pig I once was."

"No, you didn't. You didn't just pull out the pig card. You had to bring that up now. I feel bad for saying it. You were a pig when we first met, but now you're not. You have changed so much in such a short time, I wouldn't know you as the same man. So pig you are no longer, my love."

"In my eyes, I will always be that pig you first met. As long as I keep that in the back of my mind, I'll forever strive to become much more for you—strive to deserve someone like you. Yes, Tamara, I am still a pig, a pig trying to become better than he was to earn his place by you. Why do you ask about fantasies? Is there one you have?"

"Well, yes, or I wouldn't have asked. Listen to me, getting all defensive and shit. You deserve better than that. But yes, I have always enjoyed some types of bondage, but I have never been with someone I trusted enough to allow them to take dominance over me. I feel that with you, I can allow myself to indulge in these dark pleasures, as long as you're willing."

"Damn, I didn't expect that. You trust me enough to allow yourself to be submissive to me. Wow, I thought it would be a very long time until you trusted me that much. I am deeply honored. I've never done anything like that before, and I am not sure what to do, but I'm willing to do whatever you want me to do. I want to please you in any and every way possible."

"I didn't think I would ever trust deeply enough to enjoy what I am about to ask you to do. See, when I was a young girl, I had a master for a while. I trusted him with everything but one. That one I would never allow him or anyone else to do to me in fear of dying. I knew he would stop once I uttered my safe word, but deep down inside me, I didn't trust him to stop."

"Wait just a damn minute. I won't do anything that might cost you your life."

"No, David, it's not like that. There is a small danger element. That's what makes it exciting. But if you keep my safe word in the front of your mind and when you hear it, let go and everything will be fine. You need to trust me in this."

"I'm not sure. I don't want to harm you in any way, shape, or form. But if you say it's safe, then I trust that you know what you're doing and I will be your willing servant."

"Not servant. Master for at least this. I'll go get what we need and be right back."

Tamara got up and left the room just as nude as she entered and walked down to her room. A few minutes later, she came back carrying a leather strap. It was about three feet long with a circular metal ring on one end. "This is a leash. It is used to lead the submissive around with, or it can be used as a choking collar. What I want is for you to take me from behind with this around my neck and pull tight enough to cut the air supply down but not off."

"Tamara, that's nuts and very dangerous. I'm not sure I can do that. You're asking me to strangle you, to take you to the brink of life and death. That's a bit far, I think."

"If you do what I tell you and remember the safe word, I'm going to tell you everything will be fine. This will make the experience more intense for me and pleasure just as intense. The safe word must be a word that you will not be able to mistake for anything else for it has nothing to do with sex, eroticism, or anything at all, and my safe word is *translucent*. Say it."

"Translucent. I think I understand. The word must be something that I can't take for something you might say in the height of pleasure. It must be something so far apart from the experience, I won't mistake it for something you might say during an orgasm. I understand, but I am still not sure about this."

"David, please, I have been waiting my whole life to find the one man I could trust enough to put my life in his hands. I know you to be this man, and only you can do this. I really want to enjoy this experience with you and no one else. Will you please do this for me, please?"

David was still reluctant but agreed to Tamara's wishes. This meant he would bring someone to the brink of death without taking them all the way there. In some sort of twisted, messed-up way, this intrigued him. For the past week, Randolph had been telling him stories of murder, and this would allow David the chance to experience it without actually taking a life. At the same time, it would allow him to bring his lover to a level of ecstasy she so desired.

"I'll do as you want, my love. But promise me that nothing can go wrong. Promise me we'll come away from this even closer than we are now. Can you make these promises to me?"

"Yes, my loving David. Don't worry. I will be okay. Just remember the safe word and that it means to let go of the leash."

Tamara took David by the hand and led him back to the bed. She began kissing him and caressing him. She took her tongue to places David had been dreaming of. When she had David hot and worked up to the point she needed him to be, she gave him the lead end of the leash and bent over the bed. David moved behind her and gently penetrated her in the fashion she wanted. The stronger he pumped inside his beloved Tamara, the tighter he pulled on the leash.

Tamara was struggling, and this made the experience more intense for David. The more she struggled, the harder David pulled on the leash. He could feel her tighten up inside. This made it even more pleasurable. With every stroke, with each gasping sounds, the feeling became more and more intense for David. Tamara lunged back just as David was reaching maximum pleasure and was at the point of exploding inside her.

Tamara and David both slumped over onto the bed, Tamara on her face and David across her back. "That was more than I ever expected. I didn't know it could feel that way. I never imagined anything as intense as that. I hope it was even more so for you, my love. I hope it was more than you expect it to be." David ran his fingers through Tamara's hair and brushed his hand along her face. But she didn't move.

David leaned over and kissed her on the cheek, and still Tamara didn't move. She just lay there, limp with her eyes closed tight. David just sat there for a moment, not believing what was going through his head. He was thinking he had just killed the only love he had ever know. "Tamara, wake up. Please, my love, wake up. You promised me this couldn't happen. You promised me you'd be all right. That nothing could go wrong."

David lifted her to the bed and laid her down. He pulled the covers up over her and tucked them in like she was asleep. *This can't be happening*, David thought. This couldn't be. He had just killed Tamara. He took her life as she was bringing him pleasure. "How the hell could this be? How could I have allowed this? I knew this was too dangerous and it would hurt you. Why did you insist on me doing this? Why didn't you say the safe word? What went wrong?"

All this went through David's mind at once. He went from blaming himself to blaming Tamara. If only she hadn't wanted this so badly. If she would have said her safe word, then she would be alive, and David would still have her. *Well, dumb ass, you've fucked up good this time. You'll have to tell Randolph so he can call the police and a coroner. Someone has to notify her family.* Did she have any family? David waited there beside her until he heard the car drive up. It must have been near one o'clock if he was back. *I'll wash up and go downstairs to meet Randolph and give myself up to the police.*

David went into the bathroom and turned on the hot and cold water in the shower. He stood there for what seemed like hours, thinking of how this could have happened. How he wanted to join his love, but that would be the cowardly thing to do. He had never been thought of as a coward. He had put himself in harm's way too many times to count. He would do the right thing and turn himself in and face what was coming to him. He wouldn't even try to explain this. He would just say he raped her.

This would ensure he would get the maximum punishment allowed by law. For the state of Louisiana, that was death by lethal injection. This was too easy in David's mind. He deserved something even more heinous with more suffering than his beloved Tamara had experienced. David climbed into the shower as he heard the front door close. In a few minutes, he would tell Randolph what he had done, and he would call for the police.

Randolph was sitting in his usual chair when David walked into the room. "Hi, David. Sorry I wasn't here this morning for breakfast. I hope Tamara wasn't too upset after me telling her to be home in time for it." David's head hung low as he sat down in the chair beside Randolph. "What's wrong, David? Is there something you want to tell me?"

"Yes, Randolph, there is, but I'm not sure where to begin."

"Well, at the beginning has always been the best place for me. Why don't you start there?"

"Tamara is dead, Randolph, and I've killed her. So you need to call the authorities so I can give myself up."

"I'll do no such thing. This was meant to happen. It was her destiny to die at your hand."

"What are you talking about? Destiny? Don't you understand? I've killed Tamara. I fucked her and strangled her to death. Now call the damn police."

"I understand fully, David. You killed her in the heat of passion while making love to her and doing something you didn't want to do but did to please her. Am I missing anything there? Am I misunderstanding any of that?"

"How the hell did you know? It just happened. How could you

know? I see. You have cameras in my room and your sick ass watched every second of it, didn't you?"

"No, David there aren't any cameras in this house at all. I wouldn't allow them in here. I like my privacy too much to put them in the house. So no, I didn't watch you and her. Here, David, have a drink and calm down and I'll tell you all about it." Randolph poured David a stiff drink.

"Tell me all about what? What could you tell me to explain how you knew what went on? If there are no cameras, then how in the hell could you have known?" David took the glass up to his mouth and took a large gulp of the brown liquid.

"You see, David, you and I have more in common than you could ever understand. Today was meant to happen as it has so many times before."

"What are you rambling on about, Randolph, you old fool? Get off your ass and call the damn cops. I killed Tamara. Can't you get that through your fucking skull?"

"I knew you did, David, and so did I over forty years ago. See, David, I told you at the beginning I would tell you about my first two murders, about how I started killing. Now it's time."

"We don't have time for this shit, old man. Call the damn cops."

"See, David, you and I are the same. Not that we are alike, no. We are the same person but at different times. Like you, I didn't believe it until I was thrown back in time some forty years ago. I, too, was brought to this house and was forced to listen to myself ramble on about killings he committed."

"You're fucking nuts, Randolph. You've lost your ever loving mind. We are the same person? You've been watching too many sci-fi movies. Time travel doesn't exist. We can't travel back in time or I would go back and keep myself from killing Tamara."

"David, you're right. Time travel isn't possible, but a time vortex is, and that's what we're in. Some sort of time vortex that keeps looping us through time to live it over and over again."

"Damn it, Randolph, stop talking foolishness and call the cops or I'll do it myself. Stop all this time bullshit."

"Tamara is your first murder, and I'm to be the second one. In fact, you will take the gun inside the door of this table beside me, put it to my head, and pull the trigger. That's how you will end my life. Then you will take the car and leave here. That's when you're thrown back in time."

"You've gone mad if you think I'm going to kill you. I know you're dying and want to end your suffering, but I won't be the one who does it. I didn't mean to kill Tamara, but she's dead just the same and by my hand. Now call the fucking cops."

David reached for the phone sitting on the table beside Randolph and put it to his ear. He yelled into it. "Hello? Hello, hello," but there was no dial tone. "The damn thing is dead. Why isn't the phone working?"

"David, don't you remember? It has never worked. The first night you were brought here, you tried it. It didn't work then and it doesn't work now. Please sit down and listen to me. We don't have much time. Here's my wallet with all the credentials you'll need down the road."

"I don't want your wallet. I want the cops, and if you're not going to call them and I can't, I'll get Justin to take me into town and I'll turn myself in there."

David walked to the door and yelled for Justin, but he didn't answer. "Where's Justin?"

"I told him his services were no longer required and gave him severance pay. I told him I would once I no longer needed him. Now sit down and listen to me. Time is short."

David went back over to the table with the phone and tried it again, but still there was nothing. He then walked to the front door, opened it, and looked out. The car wasn't in the driveway as it was usually each day before. David ran all over the house, looking for a phone that worked, looking for Justin, and still there was just him and Randolph.

"David, please sit down. I'm telling you the truth. This has all happened many times, and it will happen many more times. There is nothing you or I can do to stop it. You have already killed Tamara, and I told you things about that only you and she could know. I've told you how you would kill me, and yet you don't believe me. I'm trying to change things, as did the Randolph I killed tried to change things. Each time we all try to change things and even stop them from occurring, and each one of us fails. This is going to happen whether or not you believe. There is nothing you can do to stop it from happening, David."

David stood there beside the table that held the gun Randolph told him about moments before. He reached his hand inside the table drawer and felt the cold plastic handle as it filled his hand. He pulled it out from the drawer and looked down at it. It was a small caliber revolver, a .38, he thought. He looked down at Randolph and asked him, "Why?"

"Why, I can't just take my own life and end this here and now. Then it will never happen again. What is stopping me from doing that?" David held the gun to his temple and squeezed the trigger. David thought he would be with his beloved Tamara and this nightmare would be over. David just stood there as nothing happened with a lost look on his face. "You old fool. You never even put any bullets in it." David pointed the gun at Randolph and pulled the trigger. To David's dismay, it fired, and the bullet struck Randolph in the side of the head.

Running toward the door of the library, David dropped the gun on the floor. David ran out the front door into the driveway. He stood there looking around, his head spinning with the thought that he had taken the lives of two people this day. He remembered the old garage and it housed an old 1960's model car. He could take it into town and turn himself in to the police then. David ran over to the old building that in the daylight looked as if it would collapse if a stiff breeze hit just right. David tried the door, and it was still locked. He walked around and looked for a way inside. He spotted the window. He stood there looking in as he had done the first night he was brought to this place. The car was still there, but did it run? Would it start?

David looked around for something to break the glass with and saw a rock just larger than his hand. He bent over and picked it up and threw it through the glass. David reached inside and unlocked the window and climbed inside the old dilapidated structure. He walked around to the driver's side of the car and opened the door. David sat down in the seat and looked around for the keys. He opened the glove compartment, hoping the keys were inside. He only found an old wallet and a letter. As he was looking frantically for the keys, his knee hit something that made a metallic clanging sound. It was the key still in the ignition. In his haste, David had overlooked the one place they should be.

David turned the key, praying it would start. The car made a rumbling sound as the motor turned over and fired up. He placed the car in reverse and pushed the gas pedal to the floor. The car jerked and raced toward the main doors. As it crashed through the old wooden doors, it splintered into thousands of pieces. David put the car in drive as soon as it was clear of the garage and sped down the dirt road that led away from the house. As he drove faster to put as much distance between him and that place, his mind kept going back to Randolph and the things he had said. How David would be thrown back in time and this was just a never-ending loop.

Randolph had been right about David killing him and knew

things that only Tamara and he could have known. But no way was there such a thing as time travel. David put those thoughts into the far reaches of his brain. David drove down the dirt road, and suddenly a thick fog rolled in. It was so thick David couldn't see anything of the road except the edges. "I'll break through this in a few seconds, then I can look for some sort of signs that tell me which way to town."

The fog wasn't easing up, and now David could barely see any part of the road. He was trying his best to keep the car going straight so he wouldn't run into a tree or something. Suddenly, David heard a loud thud and felt the car hit something. He stopped the car and got out. David looked down the road behind him and saw nothing. The fog was lifting now, and he could see more clearly. David sat back into the seat and saw the letter sitting there. He picked it and pulled the piece of paper from inside and read it.

"David, you know me as Randolph Cardigan. I was born in 1964 to parents Beatrice and Paul Erwin with the given name of David Randolph Erwin. I don't know how many times this has happened, I just know it is some sort of loop in time. If you go to the rear of the car, you'll find a small flashlight, and you can go to the right side and see what you hit. However, by now you should already know. It was the young boy I first told you about.

"No, this can't be!"

ACKNOWLEDGMENTS

Without the help and loving support of these people, Time for a Serial Killer would not have been possible.

Dustin Thomas

Terry Carlisle

Jeffery Roberts

Santa Medlin

Tasha Mullins

Stephanie Larkin

Red Penguin Books

ABOUT THE AUTHOR

R. K. Mullins was brought up in a small town in Virginia, deep in the Appalachian Mountains where he attended high school but did not graduate. He didn't learn to read beyond the fourth grade level until he was twenty-five. It has taken R. K. Mullins over ten years to write this book with special thanks to Craig Cowart, a dear friend of R.K. Mullins who pushed him to finish the book. Without his friendship, this book may have never been finished.

Thanks, Craig.

www.ingramcontent.com/pod-product-compliance
Lightning Source LLC
Chambersburg PA
CBHW071822190726
48292CB00005B/1557